♥

When a romance ends, it's hard to believe that a new love may be right around the corner. But it can be! If you've ever been in this situation—or others like it—this book is for you!

I couldn't believe it when Roger told me it was over! Only two nights before he was hugging me and telling me how happy he was! The next thing I know he's telling me he needs "space." I kept asking, "What happened?" but he just looked at me with a confused expression on his face.

It's been a few weeks now, and I still can't quite figure it out.

MEG F. SCHNEIDER lives in Riverdale, New York. She holds an M.A. in counseling psychology and has written several nonfiction books for young adults, including *Two in a Crowd: How to Find Romance Without Losing Your Friends,* also published by Pacer Books.

Other Pacer Books you will enjoy:

Two in a Crowd: How to Find Romance Without Losing Your Friends, Meg F. Schneider
Lovers' Games, Barbara Cohen
Roadside Valentine, C. S. Adler
In the Middle of a Rainbow, Barbara Girion
Vacation Fever!, Wendy Andrews
Confessions of a Teenage TV Addict, Ellen Leroe
A Very Brief Season, Barbara Girion
The Green of Me, Patricia Lee Gauch
Him She Loves?, M. E. Kerr
I'm Not Your Other Half, Caroline Cooney

Love Cycles
The Many Faces of Romance

Meg F. Schneider

Pacer BOOKS FOR YOUNG ADULTS

BERKLEY BOOKS, NEW YORK

LOVE CYCLES
THE MANY FACES OF ROMANCE

A Berkley/Pacer Book, published by arrangement
with the author

PRINTING HISTORY
Berkley/Pacer edition / November 1985

All rights reserved.
Copyright © 1985 by Meg F. Schneider
This book may not be reproduced in whole or in part,
by mimeograph or any other means, without permission.
For information address: The Berkley Publishing Group,
200 Madison Avenue, New York, New York 10016.

ISBN: 0-425-08423-X
RL: 7.6

Pacer and Two Hearts are trademarks belonging to
The Putnam Publishing Group.

A BERKLEY BOOK® TM 757,375
Berkley/Pacer Books are published by The Berkley Publishing Group,
200 Madison Avenue, New York, New York 10016.
The name "BERKLEY" and the stylized "B" with design are
trademarks belonging to Berkley Publishing Corporation.
PRINTED IN THE UNITED STATES OF AMERICA

*For Lillian, Joe, Danny and Julie with love,
and to Vicki and Lisa who have saved me on countless occasions.
To David who first touched my heart,
and to Neal who carries it with him always.*

♥ CONTENTS ♥

Introduction ix

Part I: HELPING LOVE GROW 1
Step 1: Finding the Right Person to Change With 3
Step 2: Keeping Romance Sweet 19
Step 3: Signals: Your Best Ally in Love 41

Part II: BREAKING UP IS HARD TO DO 57
Step 4: A Better Way to Break Up 59
Step 5: Sticky Breakup Situations 77

Part III: RECOVERY AND DISCOVERY! 95
Step 6: Feeling Rotten 97
Step 7: Being On Your Own 113
Step 8: Full Circle: A Fresh Beginning 129

Conclusion 145

Note From the Author 147

❤ INTRODUCTION ❤

Romance, like most other things in life, is always moving and changing. It *never* stays in one place. This can be a difficult fact to face because when it comes to romance, change can be frightening, especially when two people change in different ways. It can leave both people at first feeling quite uncertain. It may even indicate that a breakup is on the way. Little wonder that people resist change!

And therein lies the problem. It is this resistance to change, this inability to deal with new demands—fair or unfair, good or bad—that brings the most heartbreak. When romance cannot or is not allowed to move, or grow, or change, it usually ends. Quite simply, movement is the life force of romance and so it is easy to see why learning to use this "change" to your advantage is a smart move. Besides, doing so can be fun.

The constant succession of peaks and valleys in every romance can bring a lot of thrilling, difficult, rewarding, funny, warm and exciting feelings. Change, if handled well, improves and strengthens a relationship; or, if the one you are in must end, it can also set you up for a wonderful and exciting new love. Change is a fact of life, and to benefit from it, all you have to do is stay on your toes with every phase of a romance.

Romance tends to move in cycles. This is so between different relationships, as well as within one changing relationship. Usually the pattern is: the courtship phase (which is dealt with in my book *Two in a Crowd*), the established relationship phase in which the two of you grow closer, the decision making phase in which you may decide to stay together or break up, and finally, if things do end, the recovery and new beginnings stage. Each phase of the romance brings with it a host of both wonderful and trying times and changes, and each phase takes a lot of thought, awareness, and understanding of both your feelings and those of your partner. The better you are at appreciating the complicated thoughts and feelings that abound, the easier it will be to move ahead in a present relationship, or establish a new one.

There will be critical moments and periods of change in your relationship no matter how well you get along, or how much you care. Sometimes things will be better for it, sometimes you'll need to find a new partner. It's all part of the Love Cycle. But knowing how to keep a romance moving, weather the rough times, survive a break-up, and start again will make the Love Cycle work for, not against, you.

♥ PART I ♥

HELPING LOVE GROW

❤ STEP 1 ❤

Finding the Right Person to Change With

Stephanie hardly knew Peter, but she was sure he was somone she could really fall for. She'd had a crush on him for a long time. His good looks and obvious smarts made her tingle from head to toe. They were in the same chemistry class and Stephanie always made sure to sit next to him, so that they could compare homework assignments and grimace together when they faced a pop quiz. But nothing ever happened after class. Peter just picked up his books, cheerfully told her to have a nice day, and left. Finally Stephanie decided she'd had enough. One afternoon she caught him in the hallway, and invited him to join a group of friends at her house Saturday night to watch an old Hitchcock movie. Much to her surprise, he readily agreed. The evening was a huge success; Stephanie and Peter started dating. Stephanie was thrilled. She finally had the guy she wanted. Quick kisses behind the school, romantic parties, and holding hands at the movies—it was all so exciting!

But a month after they started dating Stephanie began to notice that she couldn't *really* talk to Peter. She tried to bring up important things she had on her mind about her family and her secret goals, but Peter seemed uncomfortable. He would turn the conversation back to something light. Stephanie often found herself feeling empty. There was something inside her that was ready to grow and be shared, and though she was still attracted to Peter it hurt that he was unable to see the *real* Stephanie . . .

Being "right" for each other means being happy together. It also means being able to move through the tough times together and coming out on top. The thing about "right" however, unlike what most people tend to believe, is that sometimes it is not eternal.

Two people meet, see something in each other they are attracted to, and make a decision to try and become closer. But that "thing" or "things" they were immediately interested in may not be enough to sustain a relationship. If they discover there are problems between them, it shouldn't be a surprise. In fact it's quite logical.

Romance is a gamble . . . a wonderful and exciting chance to feel those terrific sparkly sensations that go along with a lovely romance. But, it also leaves an open door for disappointment. Even the "right" guy, the one you feel happy with, may, as time moves on, become "wrong" for you. As the romance begins you just won't know.

Still, the fact remains you *can* increase the odds of picking a guy with whom you have a good chance of moving through those times of change —at least for a while—with excitement, understanding and warmth.

How Can I Tell if the Person I Like Is Someone I Can Grow With?

Sometimes you can't. Some attractions are blinding and it's hard to separate the good from the bad. That's why it's always a good idea (though sometimes it's difficult) to "take it slow." There *are*, however, certain qualities and feelings that most people agree are essential to a successful relationship.

You Can Laugh Together

Some people share a similar sense of humor. A common approach toward everyday affairs may allow you and your partner to see the humor in all kinds of circumstances. Laughing openly with another person is wonderful fun, and when people connect in this way, a natural kind of warmth and pleasure can build.

You Can Talk Honestly

Being able to talk about things that are important to you is crucial. Everyone loves to have fun, but even the class comic needs to take off his mask with someone. Relationships grow as people are able to share their innermost feelings. It's important to discover each other's needs. If you can really talk with someone, it's a sign that you're comfortable sharing your thoughts with this person.

You Can Share Interests

Shared interests can bring people together, and though on the surface it may seem that this is an impersonal reason to begin a relationship, often it isn't. Certain shared activities and interests could mean there's something quite similar about two people. Also, it's a solid foundation. Enjoying the same sport, music, subject or committee gives people an easy and comfortable common ground on which to build.

Your Partner Has Key Traits

In addition to the above elements that call for a kind of chemistry between the two of you, there are some traits you might want to look for in a romantic partner which indicate his ability to keep a relationship growing:

- **Flexibility:** Is he able to say things like, "I never thought of that. I can see your point, too, and I'm willing to go along with it"? Or is he more prone to say, "No. You're wrong. I want it my way."?
- **Understanding:** Is he able to communicate that your feelings count even if they are not the same as his?
- **Self-awareness and expression:** Can he express honest feelings? Can he look at his own behavior and say, "Boy, I guess I really did do something hurtful. I guess I was very angry," or "I feel *this* way about that because . . ."?

Without at least a little flexibility, understanding and self-awareness (on both your parts), you could find yourself involved in a frustrating, unhealthy relationship. People who don't know themselves often don't have the confidence to admit when they are right or wrong or when there are no set answers. Usually they have trouble sticking around for any amount of time . . . that is, if they aren't left first!

Humor, communication, flexibility and shared interests are important indicators that there could be something special between you and another person. Sometimes, however, your instincts can tell you to start a relationship when for the most part you're not at all sure why . . .

Things Often Seem Right at First. How Can I Tell if I Picked the Wrong Person?

Generally speaking, "wrong" reasons (or rather reasons that increase the possibility of someone being hurt), are usually ones that have more to do with you than with him. It's not *him* you like as much as the way he fills your needs.

You Find Yourself Alone

You've just broken up with someone and can't bear the loneliness you feel. Suddenly, several people whom you've known all along begin to look attractive to you.

The problem here is that attempting to make just anybody fill the space of someone who had been very special can lead to a lot of disappointment and pain.

You Feel Left Out

Everyone you know is seeing someone, and you can't bear the thought of not having someone too. Friday and Saturday night parties roll around, everyone has plans with their dates, and you're left out.

It's true that someone's presence on a double date or at a party may make you feel better. But it's when the two of you are alone and relating on a one-to-one basis that trouble can set in. If you don't have anything to share, your relationship is going to stand still—and soon fall apart.

You Feel Rejected

Vicki's Story

Steven broke up with me immediately after the prom. I couldn't believe it. The embarrassment and hurt were almost unbearable . . . especially since everyone could see that he had been flirting with Patti the whole night.

A week later Sam asked me out, and after one date the two of us plunged into an intense rela-

tionship. A month later I could tell I was just plain miserable and that Sam was feeling the same. I just wasn't there for him.

Dating someone right after another person suddenly breaks up with you can seem like a perfect way to tell someone, "I'm over you. I can like someone else." But there is a big problem with this. Your pride should never be so closely linked with another person's acceptance of you. It's dangerous to use another person in order to feel good about yourself. When the relationship ends, you may find yourself feeling badly, not just about the loss, but also about yourself!

You Have Something to Prove

Getting involved can seem like a good way to prove there's nothing wrong with you or your ability to have a relationship.

Of course, being alone doesn't mean there's something "wrong" with you. But sometimes it's easy to feel that way. When you're not ready for something that your friends are able to enjoy, you feel terrible. When your friends have found someone special and you haven't, that can make you feel awful too. And if you have recently broken up with someone and your other friends are still involved, the loneliness can be overwhelming. But try to remember that sometimes breaking up, or being on your own, can say there's something *right* about you. It takes strength to let things come to an end. And it takes independence, courage and confidence to be on your own.

The Chase

There's someone out there you want to "get," though you may not even know who he is. You are, however, obsessed.

Sometimes you may need to prove to yourself that you can have what you want. It's an ego thing. But throwing yourself into a relationship just for the sake of being involved makes it easy to lose sight of what it is you see in your partner. It's the victory, not the prize, that becomes the incentive. So, when the chase is over and reality—a relationship—sets in, things are often not what you expected. By then, it's usu-

LOVE CYCLES

ally too late to end things without someone getting hurt.

These "wrong" reasons for getting involved are often difficult to recognize at first. Your other needs may be too strong. If you suspect your motives . . . try and go slow. You may not avoid pain, but a little hurt is certainly better than a lot. Besides, a relationship that starts on shaky footing could easily turn into magic—if you think it through and give it a chance.

What About Physical Attraction? It Always Makes Me Feel So "In Love"!

Physical attraction is a very powerful thing between two people. It can make them want to spend all of their time together. But this attraction has very little to do with what each person is really like inside. Since it's what's inside a person that determines the kind of relationship you will have, physical attraction should be considered a fabulous and important thing—but *not the last word*.

Everyone needs to relate in different ways in order to grow close. Of course, there is nothing wrong with dating someone because you're attracted to him. In fact, it's extremely natural. But there's a danger of becoming too involved too quickly, before you've had a chance to get to know him. After the exciting newness of your physical intimacy wears off, the expectation is that there will be an intense emotional closeness. Emotional connections, however, don't work that way. They develop at different rates, and for different reasons, than physical relationships. Thus, when people who have been physically close start searching for the personal communication to match, they often find themselves empty-handed. Sometimes, if you give it time, the nearness develops. But usually it's too painful, confusing and disappointing to hang in there and wait. So people break up.

A physical attraction is no less sincere or true than any other attraction. But sometimes it seems to promise more than it can ever amount to.

What if I Think He Is Right For Me But He Doesn't Think So?

Warren's Story

Diane and I had been dating casually for a while and I really thought that we could have something going. We usually got together every Friday night and went to the movies or to a party. I thought we were having a great time, but I sensed Diane was losing interest. She started dating different guys and I could tell they didn't make her all that happy. Her relationships ended soon enough. But still she just wanted to be my friend.

It made me miserable. I just couldn't imagine how anyone could be better for me . . .

Just because you think someone is right for you doesn't automatically make you right for them. But it also doesn't mean that, given a little time, one or both of you won't change your minds. If you both come to feel that you should get together, that's great. But if you never seem to get it together, there are a few things about being "right" that are important to remember.

First of all, *many people can be right for you*. This is hard to believe when you're in love, but the truth is you could be happy with someone else. Every person has many sides to their personality, one of which you may find attractive. With each new encounter, you may find that different people have different sets of exciting ideas and attitudes to bring to a relationship. Remember, because we all are unique, we each have our own special something to offer!

Secondly, being *right* for somone is subject to change. Someone who once regarded you as being "right" for them may have a change of heart. This may or may not have something to do with you. Often it is difficult to determine the reasons why the relationship is not working.

Caring strongly for someone who does not return the feeling in the same way is painful. It is a very common experience, and no one enjoys it. But it is important to recognize that it does not indicate that anything is wrong with you, but rather it reflects the differences between you and your partner. Often people want different things out of their relationship, and the imbalance of expectations alone is enough to throw the romance off kilter. Frequently, outside influences make it a bad time to get involved. Emotional preoccupations can weigh heavily on a person, with the commitment of a relationship threatening to be the last straw. Try not to let your feelings of rejection take over. Just look around for somone who is ready to get close.

If you want a relationship, you have to take your chances. But it's not as out of your control as it sounds. Awareness of yourself while in a relationship, an awareness of the person you are involved with, is crucial. You might pay attention to how you help each other grow and how you may inhibit one another. By recognizing the problems you share, you can work together to find constructive ways to deal with them. This kind of teamwork shows you care and reaffirms that both of you feel the relationship is worthwhile.

♥ STEP 2 ♥
Keeping Romance Sweet

Linda and Ted had been dating for a while, and they fell in love. However, there was one problem in their relationship which continued to crop up. Ted was working very hard in school to achieve good grades for college. He was anxious to be a doctor and wanted to get into the best school possible. Linda was proud of Ted's ambition, but found that his long study hours often got in the way of their having a good time. On many occasions, Linda had to go to basketball games, movies, and tennis matches with her girlfriends and their boyfriends. She even attended a party or two without him!

Usually, the day after Linda and Ted spent

the evening apart, they would argue. Linda felt frustrated and lonely and Ted felt the pressure of trying to balance his work and his love life. Both were so hurt they found it difficult to listen to each other. They wanted to stay together, but things just weren't going along the way they expected.

True love, or even just "liking a lot" is not a simple matter. It's a wonderful thing, but it isn't easy. And expecting it will be is the quickest way to a speedy break up.

Keeping romance alive can be tricky. Potentially difficult moments will crop up. Unexciting times will appear. If your affection is real then the working out of these problems should become as uncomplicated as your attraction for each other.

Disagreements and misunderstandings are as much a part of a love relationship as kissing and warm conversation. Still, of course, it's always nice to try and keep them at a minimum. This does not mean you should hide angry feelings, but rather, that you should communicate in such a way that the anger is understood and talked out.

It gets down to preventive measures. There are a number of things to keep in mind when embarking on a relationship that could fend off quite a bit of trouble . . .

• • •

How Can I Keep the Excitement in Our Romance? Sometimes It Just Seems to Disappear.

To begin with, *you* alone cannot keep the excitement in your relationship. Romantic excitement is the pleasure and responsibility of *two* people.

Secondly, exciting times will come and go, and then come again. That is the nature of life. And in a way it's just as well. We do have to function in a practical world, and if we were to constantly walk around with our heads spinning we'd be in very big trouble. Look at Romeo and Juliet! No romance is an ongoing journey of pure excitement. Quiet times, gentle moments, and even monotonous days will occur. It doesn't mean romance is over. It just means that you, your partner and the excitement between you are at rest.

Thirdly, despite the fact that one should never look for thrills every moment, there are things you can do to help keep your romance captivating:

- *Don't* take his affections for granted. It's easy to become sloppy with another person's feelings when confident of their affections. But don't do it. Everyone needs to feel cared for. If your partner feels that he is no longer special, he may look elsewhere for that reassurance.

- *Don't* allow yourselves to fall into routines. Always going to the same place with the same friends can become boring. A change in atmosphere where you can experience new things and meet new people will give your romance an exciting flavor.
- *Don't* panic if your partner says, "Things don't feel as exciting as before." Instead, stay calm, and ask him what he thinks the two of you should do about it. If you don't turn his observation into a nightmare, it won't become one. Chances are the two of you will think of just the right alluring something to put the thrills back where they belong.
- *Do* find ways to consistently express your caring. Occasional compliments, sweet little gifts or thoughtful favors will let him know you think he's special and that this romance deserves attention.
- *Do* think up surprises! Plan an evening and don't tell him what it is. Just take him there! Miniature golf, an old Hitchock film, or a night of ice-skating under the stars—it's not what you do, but how you do it!

- *Do* remember that excitement can be encouraged . . . but that it can't be manufactured. Setting the stage for romantic excitement is easy enough to do, and often it works. But occasionally it won't. Self-conscious attempts to make things "work" will often come off as forced and unnatural. Sometimes, if you just accept the absence of excitement it will reappear on its own later. Other times it won't. Either way, it's not a sign of success or failure. It's just there or it isn't, and you'll either decide to continue the relationship or you won't. Whatever way you go, in this relationship or the next, excitement will be yours again!

Can I Express My Angry and Hurt Feelings and Still Come Out On Top?

The best way to minimize the rough times is to face your feelings. By exposing both positive and negative feelings, you gain a clearer understanding of your emotions. Keeping misunderstandings, grudges and bad feelings to yourself will only serve to aggravate you. Then things that aren't meant will be said, and feelings that don't deserve to be hurt will be crushed.

Here's a five-part plan for expressing your feelings while being careful of his:

- *Rule #1:* Don't assume your partner knows what you mean. Suppose you and your boyfriend are singing to the radio. Listening to him sing out of tune makes you laugh and you say, "Oh you're terrible!" What you really meant by these words was, "You're so adorable," but your boyfriend, who is already sensitive about his terrible voice, takes it as an insult.

  Think about what you say, and try to put yourself in his shoes. Be sensitive to how teasing words can sound. If you have trouble seeing his sensitive spots, tell him he really must clue you in. Otherwise, you may unintentionally say something painful.

  When people feel cared for they feel more confident, and it makes it easier for honest feelings to emerge.

- *Rule #2:* Never, but never, tell your partner that he is being ridiculous. Instead, *listen*. Hear what is being expressed and try to understand. Whether it's a problem between the two of you or something completely unrelated to the relationship, people need and want to be understood. Otherwise, they feel lonely. Loneliness in a relationship can turn into anger, and anger brings on those bad times. So give your partner's feelings credit. Chances are you'll get the same respect in return.

- *Rule #3:* If something significant happens in your relationship and it bothers you, don't ignore it. Express it. Otherwise, it will fester, and if the situation occurs again, big trouble will hit the scene. The important thing to keep in mind here, however, is to communicate your distress in a non-accusatory way. You'll get a lot further with, "I'm sure you didn't mean to hurt me, but the other day when you———I felt terrible," than you will with a "You behaved very selfishly the other day. I felt so rotten when you———." Dealing with small problems in a sensitive way will keep them from spiraling into a furious mess. Try not to accuse your partner and cause him to put up his defenses. Lastly, don't collect ill feelings. It's a lot easier to handle bad feelings in small doses than it is when things really blow up.
- *Rule #4:* Always to be open to the possibility that you may be wrong or that

there is no right or wrong. Many times people feel hurt or angry over something, and they are entitled to these feelings. However, it doesn't mean that what they expect or want is fair. Wanting your boyfriend to go shopping with you and your friends when he would prefer to go to a football game with his buddies is a good example. Shopping is important to you. The football game is important to him. Who's right? Sometimes you have to call it a draw and just let the other person be.

- *Rule #5:* Don't pretend to be someone you are not. If something bothers you, it bothers you. If you enjoy something in particular, then that is what makes you happy. And if you're sensitive about something, then that may be your sore spot. Plain and simple. Trying to be someone you are not to please your partner *never ever* works. In the end you can only be happy if your personal needs are being met. You may be able to hide from another person, but you can't hide from yourself. And if you can bravely ask for what you need, you just may get it! So be sure to communicate your feelings, both positive and negative, and above all be honest!

• • •

LOVE CYCLES

What Is Fair to Expect from a Romance?

Lisa's Story

Dennis and I always go out after school on Fridays for pizza. It has become a kind of ritual between us. But last Wednesday, Dennis called up to tell me that he wouldn't be able to make it this Friday. One of his friends invited him to join an impromptu basketball game and he really wanted to go. I felt gypped and asked him why he couldn't play some other afternoon. Dennis explained that this was the only day that all the guys could make it. He told me that he called early so that I would have time to make other plans.

Other plans! I couldn't believe it! I muttered some kind of quick goodbye, hung up and wondered to myself how come things were going down the drain when just yesterday he told me how much he cared . . .

Everyone enters a relationship with expectations. But relationships, just like people, can be somewhat unpredictable. Often things people really look forward to in a relationship don't happen quite as expected. Phone conversations aren't as long, laughter isn't as frequent, everything isn't shared. But on the other hand, things people never anticipated needing, such as a partner with a lot of patience, are suddenly theirs . . . and they love it!

It's really rather unfair to both people to enter into a relationship with *specific* expectations. To make a number of inflexible demands on someone's personality that simply don't suit that person's emotions or way of thinking can lead to trouble. Besides, no one likes to feel as though they have to do everything "right"!

There are many things you can expect from a romantic relationship, but the degree to which you ask for or anticipate them is where the trouble may begin. Each person you are involved with will have different interests, strengths and beliefs and therefore will only be able to meet your needs in accordance with who they are. To ask for more would be to ask for another person.

A Sharing of Interests

One of the best things about a relationship is the exciting feeling of having someone to be with. Having fun doing things together is wonderful, and naturally you will want to introduce your boyfriend to all the different activities you enjoy. However, don't overwhelm him with your enthusiasm. He may take to some of your hobbies and make them his own, but don't expect him to love all the same things you do. As long as he appreciates and respects your interests and allows you the time to pursue them, this is all you can rightfully ask.

Understanding

Bill's Story

Maggie and I had been dating for months and were known as a very solid couple. Everyone envied us. But one afternoon, Maggie became very upset over a grade she'd gotten on a paper. When she tried to share her misery with me, I guess I wasn't as sympathetic as she'd expected. She kept pushing the issue and getting more upset, until she just plain wouldn't listen to me. I explained that I understood she felt bad, but that I just couldn't consider it the tragedy of a lifetime.

Horrified that I didn't seem to understand her

anymore, Maggie decided it was time to date other people. I didn't like it . . . but what could I do?

It's understandable to expect your partner to be supportive. People who become emotionally and physically close tend to rely on each other for warmth and understanding. If one person is upset, it's fair to expect the other will be there to offer comfort. But to expect that every problem—even small, solvable ones—is going to be met with complete understanding and patience is unreasonable. Not everyone is going to view your situation as a problem.

Differences of opinion, or the way in which you or your boyfriend may interpret a situation, are bound to occur. This does not mean that either one of you has failed the other. It only means that each of you sees the world through your own eyes. Usually it is the way your partner looks at life that attracts you to him in the first place. So when a problem arises treat your partner with kindness and respect. It's okay to explain, "I don't understand why you feel this way, but clearly you do and I'm sorry you feel hurt."

• • •

Honesty and Respect

Relationships can be a serious affair. While building a romance, you and your partner will begin to reveal the feelings you have for one another. This stage can be frightening for both parties. Not knowing how your boyfriend feels about you makes it difficult to share such personal emotions. There is always the fear that he does not feel the same way about you. Nobody likes to feel vulnerable, and this is why it is important to always treat your partner with respect. Laughing at or ignoring his feelings after he has trusted you enough to self-disclose can be the cause of much mean and unnecessary heartache.

However, respect also requires honesty. Both need to work hand-in-hand for a healthy relationship to evolve. It is important for each of you to know the other can be trusted to speak the truth. If ever there is a time you feel unhappy, tell your partner. Together, through open communication, you should be able to arrive at a solution.

• • •

What Are "Unreasonable" Expectations?

People involved in romance often expect fairy tales. But relationships exist in the real world, and so our expectations have to live there too. Below is a collection of the most "unreasonable" expectations that are guaranteed to ruin just about any relationship.

Constant Togetherness

People need time away from each other. This includes husbands and wives, brothers and sisters, and even best friends. Too much togetherness stunts your growth as individuals. People grow by moving out into the world alone and enjoying for themselves all the different kinds of experiences and relationships that await them. Wanting time to yourself by no means undermines the love you feel for your partner.

• • •

Always Wanting to be #1

Sasha's Story

I was planning to go bicycling with my boyfriend Willie on Saturday morning. The plans had been set for days. But when Saturday morning arrived, Willie called to say his best friend Jake had just broken up with his girl and really needed to talk to him. I was so disappointed that I insisted he go biking with me, since our plans were longstanding. I guess Willie was so surprised by my strong reaction that he gave in.

After biking a few miles, we pulled over to the side of the road to buy a couple of sodas. During our break, Willie began to pick on the way my hair looked. Needless to say, I got defensive and a huge fight broke out that took all afternoon to resolve.

Of course, Jake was the topic of conversation...

When two people are involved, they often feel that their romantic partner should be the most important figure in their lives. It's true a relationship is tremendously significant, and in the arena of romance you may indeed be number one. But in other arenas, such as friendship and family responsibilities, there are other very important people to consider. Understand that you are not the only person who values, needs and loves your partner. To be able to share the attention of your boyfriend or girlfriend with another person and remain supportive is a sure sign of both maturity and compassion.

Love That Conquers All

When you first enter into a relationship, it is easy to regard it as something mystical. Looking at love as a fairy-tale romance can set you up for a terrible disappointment. Love cannot conquer all. There are problems in life that you as a person must work out on your own. Love can, however, make bad times seem more tolerable.

It takes two people to create love. And, while love does indeed feel like a magical thing, it exists in the real world. Ordinary people in the real world are going to have difficulties that have nothing to do with their love for each other. In fact, expecting that they can count on each other or on their love to take away pain or to dissolve a difficult situation will only serve to allow the *real* world to take away the *magic*. Not the other way around.

He Should Put Your Needs Before His

This is a tremendously poetic goal which true love, at times, accomplishes. However, it's an exceedingly tall order to fill. When you really love someone, there will be times when you will put aside your own desires to please your mate. And it will come from the heart. But it doesn't mean that if your boyfriend doesn't place your feelings before his, that he loves you any less.

The particulars of the situation and the tenor of your relationship must be considered first. If it seems that he's never willing to compromise his needs to fulfill yours, then there is a problem. But if he is usually fair about meeting your needs and only on occasion does not accommodate your request, perhaps you should re-evaluate what you are asking. It could be you want too much of him.

You may feel that proof of a strong couple is their willingness to put each other first. But the real proof lies with both of your abilities to listen to one another and to be *flexible!*

Is Your Partner Perfect?

If you begin to love someone assuming they are "perfect" you are definitely heading for major league trouble. No one can ever be that. There is not a person on earth who can be precisely as attractive, funny, intelligent, kind, patient or any number of other things we know we'd like or definitely think we need.

And thinking we need is the key here. Often we create a person in our minds fashioned from the things we think we need. We decide the person we are involved with is that dream, and upon discovering he is not, we become consumed by disappointment and blinded to whatever he does have that's very wonderful.

But if you remain even a little open, you may discover you don't need to find an exact specific combination of traits in another person in order to be happy. A person's most important value lies in his or her own special unique combination of qualities. What counts is the way a person takes hold of you, effects you, inspires you to care. But no one, inside and out, will ever please you in every way. (In fact, if they do, chances are you don't know the person in question very well!)

• • •

How Can I Lower My Expectations? I Can't Seem to Help Wanting Everything.

It's not easy to "let go" of dreams or expectations, and there's really no need to do so entirely. Holding on to them often helps us to strive for what we truly want instead of settling for something that isn't even close.

The problem arises, however, when we can't look past our dreams and see that we are dealing with a person and not just a thought. If you are caught up in having the ideal romance, chances are no one will seem good enough. After all, we all have faults.

The only way to experience an exciting, satisfying romance is to try and give your partner a chance. It's easy to feel trapped or disappointed or confused when we're let down, but it doesn't mean that you have to start moving at the first sign of trouble! Don't panic, the door is always open! First take the time to give a good, long look at what's going on. You may find that your demands are unrealistic. Perhaps you are passing judgment on actions you don't understand. Allow yourself the time to explore a relationship with someone who may not be what you had dreamed. You may find you'll be very pleasantly surprised!

• • •

How Do I Know How Much to Give?

The most important thing to understand about giving and taking (other than the fact that you must do both) is, never keep a ledger sheet. Everyone gives and takes in different ways at different times. To feel indebted to your partner takes away from the pleasures of receiving. To make your partner feel like he owes you one is to defy the good nature of giving.

But What if I Feel That I'm Giving Too Much?

The feeling of giving too much is not a happy one. It's usually characterized by a sense of emptiness and often loneliness. If you're giving too much, chances are you're not taking enough. That can leave you feeling sad and angry. Giving in too often and thinking more about his feelings than your own simply doesn't feel good.

But you can change the pattern, and here are some suggestions how:

- Tell him how you feel. It's a fact about human nature that we tend to want as much as we can get. If you point out what's going on, he may stop all his taking and start giving a little himself.
- Tell him what you want or need. Lots of times we expect people to read our minds, and when they don't we feel hurt and angry. This is very unfair. If you have a need that is not being fulfilled, tell him. If you want your suggestion to carry more weight, explain your feelings to him so that he can understand.
- If he doesn't realize how much he's been asking of you, then show him. The next time he asks you for something or presents you with a situation where you have to give too much, say something like, "This is what I mean. I know you don't think this is asking a lot of me, but please think about how I feel."

Every relationship is different and, therefore, should never be compared to your romance. Some people feel more comfortable giving, while others are natural takers. It is for you to decide how you feel best in your relationship. So let your heart measure what's a satisfactory give and take balance, not a ledger.

It's always a good idea to be aware of the

roots of trouble. If you know what they are, chances are you won't feed them. If you don't feed them, they will remain only potential sources of trouble, and will not grow into the real thing.

Honesty, clear communication, reasonable expectations and an open mind are your best allies in finding and enjoying a successful and exciting relationship. People can only be who they are. If you are true to yourself and allow other people the space to show you everything they can be, romance will bloom and grow almost every time.

❤ STEP 3 ❤

Signals: Your Best Ally In Love

Jessica had been seeing Peter for a few months, and things had been very nice. Everything felt romantic and warm and, other than a few minor arguments, it seemed that they really got on well together.

About a month or two ago, Jessica began to sense a tension in the air. Peter seemed to be growing a little distracted. He would arrive late at her house, sometimes make plans with other friends for afternoons the two of them usually spent alone together, and suddenly burst into brief tempers over almost nothing.

Frightened that the relationship was in trouble, she asked him if anything was the matter but, much to her relief, he assured her he just had "things" on his mind. Slightly confused, Jessica didn't press him, but she did begin acting increasingly more possessive.

Finally, one night Peter walked her home from a movie and, upon hesitating on the doorstep, he blurted out that it was over. He wanted to be on his own again.

Shocked, Jessica ran into the house, fell onto her bed, and began to cry from the very sudden hurt of it all.

No one likes bad news. It's a lot more pleasant to enjoy the fine and loving things life has to offer. But, unfortunately, bad news and rough times do occur and must be handled. Ignoring the signs that problems are on their way (and usually there *are* signs) will only serve to turn a gentle clash into a full-blown problem. Don't overlook these signs in hope that they'll take care of themselves—they won't!

Once you sense that something is wrong, the feeling will stay with you. At first it may seem an unwanted intruder, but in the end it's really your greatest protection. If there is a problem, you can rest assured it won't go away until it's sorted out. Had Jessica had a little more confidence in her instincts, things might have turned out differently.

Not facing up to a problem in an effort to avoid

a difficult conversation can lead to a sudden, painful and irreparable breakup. Discussing problems, however, can save the relationship. Small issues are a lot easier to sort out than big ones!

If you seem destined to break up, it makes a lot more sense to stay on top of things. Being aware of changes in your relationship gives you the opportunity to have some control over what happens and how it happens, and to be prepared for the results. (Being on your own can be frightening or exciting, and it all depends on how you greet it.)

By following the signals, you'll give yourself a chance to see what is happening and help yourself understand why. You'll also give yourself the chance to figure out how you can improve things. But most of all, you'll spare yourself from that horrible moment when, to your complete surprise, someone you care about calls it quits.

What Kind of Signs Am I Looking for?

- You have difficulty talking: When two people no longer connect, uncomfortable silences or empty conversations surface. Occasionally, of course, this happens to everyone. In fact, people in general need to grow more at ease with quiet times. However, prolonged periods of silence can result in a failure to communicate.

- You find yourself preferring to make plans with your friends: There will always be times at which you'd rather see a good friend than a romantic partner. You may need a bit of confidential conversation, or a good friend's insights. But sometimes, because having a romance seems so important, you may not want to face the fact that it's not giving you what you need. As a result, you seek out your friends to fill in the gaps. They can't, of course. Romance can give you things no other relationship can. Sooner or later, you'll have to face what is missing and either try to resolve it, or break up.

- You choose to see your boyfriend in group situations: Sometimes, when there are communication problems between people, they are only comfortable in crowds. They attempt to surround themselves with people so that the problem is not so obvious. Needing other friends to mask the fact that you and your partner don't have a lot to say to each other, or are avoiding necessary conversation, is hazardous. Certainly the ploy can't work for too long.

LOVE CYCLES 45

- You're interested in other guys: Seeing another person who you think is sexy, or enjoying a little romantic fantasy, does *not* mean there's something wrong with your relationship. Everyone, whether they're involved or not, notices other attractive people. It's the degree to which you'd like to follow up on this attraction that counts. If you feel there are other people out there you'd like to get to know, it may be a signal that you're feeling a need to move on.
- You feel like arguing a lot: A few fights here and there are healthy. Arguing is a form of communication, but constant bickering is something else. Usually it's a sign that the two of you are no longer compatible, or that one or both of you have negative feelings that you never sort out. Often people resort to arguing as an excuse to break up. Things are changing and it's too confusing to understand or put into words. Arguing encourages a more understandable and solid reason for separating. (Bickering can also occur due to problems unrelated to the relationship; difficulties at home, at school, etc. Sharing these concerns is important. Keeping them from each other can cause an un-

mendable rift in the relationship, where misunderstandings can spiral into terrible fights.)
- You find yourself acting in ways that aren't really you: Dissatisfaction, coupled with the feeling of being trapped, can turn a very sweet person into a grump, and an "up" personality into a real "downer." Such turnabouts generally make *everyone* involved suffer. It's no fun being on the receiving end of a sudden bad temper or cruel remark. But it's also utterly devastating to watch yourself behave in a way that *you* can't stand. Lying about your plans, flaring up at a simple misunderstanding, or angrily saying something *you know* will hurt the other person is a firm indication that you are not happy, and that something has to be done.

A long meaningful conversation or cooling of the relationship may resolve these problems. Openness can result in the two of you becoming closer. Then again, even with these measures, the signals could turn out to be preludes to a breakup. It's very unpredictable. But one thing is for sure, ignoring what is wrong in your relationship won't make it go away.

How Can I Tell if He's Unhappy?

Sometimes it's difficult to determine if your boyfriend is unhappy with the relationship or if it's something outside of your involvement that's causing him to feel bad. The following signals may be indicators that your romance is in trouble:

- He begins making up excuses for not being able to see you. Possibly he's indicating that he needs some space, that he's feeling uncomfortable with you, or that there are problems unrelated to you!
- He seems to be picking arguments with you. He could be angry at something else and taking it out on you, or he could be feeling that he needs some room and doesn't know how to tell you, so he's angry.
- You've caught him in some lies. When he was supposed to be doing his homework, he was really out bumming around with the guys. It's possible he feels you never understand his occasional need to hang out with his pals, or there's a chance he's trying to tell you that he'd like to have his freedom.
- He suddenly starts encouraging you to make plans with other people and to be

more independent. Excessive dependence in a relationship can make one or both people feel boxed in. In his own way he may be trying to loosen things up a bit, or he may be trying to prepare you for what *he* feels is an inevitable breakup.
- Loving patterns take a change for the worse. Sometimes, the simplest things—fewer phone calls or affectionate words—can tell you something isn't right. It could mean he's preoccupied with other problems, or it could be his way of communicating a change in his feelings, be it temporary or permanent.

Whatever the signal you receive, be careful not to blow the situation out of proportion. Signals do not necessarily mean that something is over. If a sign occurs once, it could be a mood or even a mistaken impression on your part. If signals do appear two or three times, they may be a warning that something in your relationship needs a bit of work.

LOVE CYCLES

How Can I Get Through the Rough Times Without Breaking Up?

Kelly's Story

I had been feeling terrible about the way things were going with Luke. It seemed that no matter what we did, where we did it, what we said and how we said it, we'd end up tense or unhappy. I could tell there was something about each other that we were still attracted to, but the problem wouldn't go away. Finally we decided to chance a trial separation. We saw each other occasionally for a couple of weeks. We even dated other people.

And you know what? It could have gone either way. Sometimes I missed him, sometimes I didn't, but we got back together anyway. I don't know if it will last, but the separation did help. We realized that what we have together is special . . .

There is no sure-fire way to get past a rough time together. But you can tip the odds in your favor. You have to be open to conversation and be willing to give each other as much *time* and *space* as you can comfortably afford. (Too much space might be too painful for one of you. This can signal that the timing for the relationship is off.) The truth is, if you don't give time and space, if you can't stretch your own needs and feelings to accommodate the other person's, chances are the relationship will steadily and quickly move downhill. True, even if you do manage the distancing successfully, things could still come apart. But it's important to try and give each other the room to think. No one likes to feel boxed in or controlled.

When talking with each other about your problems, try to keep these points in mind:

- Nobody should be accused of being "wrong."
- People cannot help the way they feel.
- Someone else's sensitivity should never be labeled "silly."
- If you can't agree, don't say you do. Call it a draw. Lying causes other problems.
- Learn to say "I'm sorry." Apologizing when you've been wrong shows your strength, not your weakness.
- Don't list faults and don't dredge up old arguments that were settled long ago.

No one can be sure when they enter a difficult conversation that they will emerge from the experience with pleasing results. But if you're not willing to be honest, listen, see your own faults and appreciate how someone else might feel, then you might as well not expect much.

Is There Any Definite Way to Tell the Difference Between a Rocky Time and Time to Break Up?

There are some general indications that to most would signal that a breakup is the best idea—whether it's to be considered permanent or a "trial" separation. (Often it's easier to think of it as the latter, as long as you don't fall into the trap of "waiting" to resume, instead of getting on with your life):

- Ongoing discussions about problems in the relationship seem to go in circles: Communication problems of this nature usually mean that people are unwilling or unable to deal with each other's feelings. Relationships cannot exist without mutual effort and understanding.
- Agreements about issues are reached, but then they are repeatedly broken: For instance, you've agreed to see other people every once in a while, but to stay away from each other's friends. Then one of you finds yourself on a date with a person your steady hangs out with. Sometimes people want a relationship, but they aren't ready to sacrifice for it. It's doesn't mean the affection is missing. It just means

that other needs are much stronger. It may mean that the "rules" you two have set up are too strict and need to be softened a bit.

- Feelings of tension and unhappiness when you're together won't go away: Sometimes there are several problems that mix with one another in such a way that it's hard to put your finger on exactly what is wrong. You simply know that something is upsetting you and it's not going away.
- You feel restless even though the affection in the relationship is still there: Just because people feel they have to move on doesn't mean their caring for each other has disappeared. Sometimes, experiencing new things and moving on is more important and necessary to a person's happiness than staying with one romance . . .
- One of you expresses the desire to date someone else: If your boyfriend has the eye for someone new, you may be tempted to hang in there while he "gets it out of his system." It's easier to remove yourself from the scene. If he is going to realize that it is you he really wants, he'll discover it whether you're dating or not. "Out of sight, out of mind" only holds when a relationship wasn't strong enough to begin with.

- Personal problems keep getting in the way of your relationship: Serious problems at home or school or other personal obligations can represent obstacles. Sometimes you can get past these problems. Other times, they have a profound effect on someone's ability to relate to another. People may adore each other, but if the "situation" isn't right, it may not work.

When it's time to call it quits, you'll know it somewhere inside. Don't be afraid of making a mistake. If you should break up and you don't, it'll just happen later and perhaps be a little more difficult. If you shouldn't break up and you do, chances are you'll find each other again!

What Am I Supposed to Think When Things Are Great, There Are No Signals, and Pow! He Wants to Break Up?

Lynn's Story

I couldn't believe it when Roger told me it was over! Only two nights before he was hugging me and telling me how happy he was! The next thing I know he's telling me he needs "space." I kept asking, "What happened?" but he just looked at me with a confused expression on his face.

It's been a few weeks now, and I still can't quite figure it out.

You might want to blame it on something called "fear of closeness." When two people grow close, they also grow to depend on each other, trust one another, and share intimate thoughts and feelings. Most people, in their less involved everyday relationships, keep a big part of themselves secret and protected. But in a romance, a big part of these secrets are brought out. Each person sees the other's more vulnerable side. The side that's most sensitive. The side that can really hurt. Sometimes exposing these innermost feelings can be terrifying.

When people who are afraid of closeness find themselves loving too much, enjoying themselves a little too frequently or needing the other a lot, fear can set in. They are afraid of being hurt. Lots of times they are not consciously aware of their fear. They just find that their emotions have shut down without their really knowing why.

This shutdown is upsetting for both people because it usually happens right after sharing a particularly close moment. However, patience and understanding can bring the person around. By being there for your partner during his retreat, you can show him that you can respect who he is and what he needs. Pressure will only add to his anxiety and convince him that an involvement with you is a scary, uncomfortable "thing."

Fear of closeness is not a sign of weakness, nor is it a flaw. It is an indication that someone is not quite ready to take a chance and "give" of themselves to another person. They need to feel safe and protected for a little while longer.

There's nothing wrong with this. You and your boyfriend should grow close at a pace that feels comfortable to you both.

Signals are tricky things. Sometimes they can be a painless way of expressing a problem, sometimes they can help inspire a much needed conversation, or sometimes, if they are misread, they can be flat out destructive. Whatever they may be, signals should not be ignored. They are saying something and relationships hardly *ever* end without them.

❤ **PART II** ❤

BREAKING UP IS HARD TO DO

❤ STEP 4 ❤
A Better Way to Break Up

A few months ago, Mary met Glenn at a party. She couldn't take her eyes off of him, and shortly thereafter the two of them became involved.

A month ago, Mary began to feel dissatisfied. She dropped subtle hints, but Glenn never seemed to pick them up. The two of them just weren't communicating. Mary was quickly losing interest in Glenn, especially after meeting Jeff at her cousin's house.

Finally, tired of pretending things were okay, Mary met Glenn at a coffee shop and told him it was over. She explained that she liked him a lot but she just didn't feel the same about him as she used to. She also added she was interested in someone else.

Hurt and angry, Glenn sat through her remarks, and when she was finished he threw some change on the table, got up and left without another word.

Saying goodbye to a romantic partner can be sad, confusing, angering and often painful. No matter how rough the course of the relationship, breaking up is an unpleasant experience.

If you're doing the breaking up, guilt over hurting your partner is often involved. There is also the fear of making the wrong decision and being alone; anxiety over handling the breakup well; and confusion over the sadness you feel, even though you're sure you did the right thing. If you're being broken up with, you can feel hurt over being left; fearful of being alone; insecure about what's "not right" about you; angry over the way the breakup was handled; or sad about losing someone you were not quite ready to let go.

The gamut of emotions both of you may experience is endless and often difficult. Whether they are handled well or badly, breakups are usually not a cause for celebration. But with a little extra understanding, patience and thought, breaking up *can* be less of a traumatic experience and much more of a meaningful, although difficult, graduation to an exciting new time in your life.

I Never Know What to Say When I Want to Break Up With Someone. Is There Something I Should Know?

One important thing to remember is that complete honesty may not be the best policy. Sometimes the situation will require the absolute truth, but most times it won't. Clearly, there's no way you can break up with someone and have them walk away from the conversation saying, "Gee, she handled that wonderfully. I feel great!" But too much honesty can be very hurtful.

There are ways to express the many kinds of feelings you may have that will: 1) be less painful to hear; 2) be easier for you to say; 3) create as few hard feelings as possible; and 4) not stand in the way of a possible reconciliation (something you may not think you want . . . but you never know . . .) .

Since breakups often happen when people still care for each other, it's a good idea to approach the separation with thoughtfulness. Impulsive breakups are often accompanied by careless remarks that cause a great deal of harm to both people *and* their memory of each other. Think then, before you speak, and consider these options.

If You're Feeling: I have nothing in common with you.
Then Try Something Like: "I feel like we're growing in different directions . . . as though we're very different people." To say you have nothing in common is probably untrue, and would seem to imply that all along there was nothing important between you.

If You're Feeling: I really don't like you anymore.
Then Try Something Like: "My feelings are changing. I care about you, but right now I need to be on my own." This approach will communicate that you want to break up without making your partner feel rejected or unloved.

If You're Feeling: I still care for you, but something isn't right, and we can't seem to make it go away. I can't stand it!
Then Try Something Like: "I still care for you a lot, but I just feel that something isn't right and no matter what we do it doesn't go away." There's nothing wrong with not know-

LOVE CYCLES 63

ing the exact reasons you want to break up. Just be sure that all you relay is your confusion. If you try to explain your feelings about a situation you don't understand, you may become frustrated and say something you don't mean.

If You're Feeling: I want to break up but I'd still like to go out with you sometime.
Then Try Somethng Like: "I feel that we have to break up, but I'm going to miss you. Do you think we can still spend a little time together once in a while?" When a relationship is over, there is a sense of loss. Time spent with the other person is now empty, spent alone. Some people will welcome a chance to see their ex, while others feel it would be too painful. Respect your ex's decision and understand that there is a reason why they have made that choice.

If You're Feeling: I like you but I'll never fall in love with you.
Then Try Something Like: "I like you a lot, but I'm not ready to become more involved." If you're questioned more closely, try to stick to the issue of what you're *ready* for, not *how you feel*. You don't have to fall in love with everyone you date. Sometimes it's nice to enjoy the person just for who they are without

considering what kind of relationship you should anticipate.

Again, breakups are complicated because the reasons they occur are *never* simple.

What if My Partner Won't Accept That the Relationship Is Over?

During a breakup, the person who's experiencing the most hurt usually feels desperate for an explanation. Talking it over with your ex can often be of some comfort. But too much rehashing of what went wrong in your relationship can sometimes prove to be a waste of time. What happened between the two of you is in the past and can't be changed. It may fall on you to help him see this fact clearly. So if he says:

"Is there something about me you don't like?" don't make a list. Simply say, "No, it's not you. It's me. I feel that I have to be on my own now." Emphasize that the decision comes from inside of you, *not* in reaction to your ex. When it gets right down to it, that's the truth anyway.

"Can't we try it again, give it some more time?" If you're sure about how you feel, *don't give in*.

LOVE CYCLES

Try saying something like, "I can't. I've given it a lot of thought because I *do* have feelings for you, but I know that it's just not working now." Whatever you do, steer away from saying, "Maybe we'll get back together," even if it *is* how you feel. Suggesting that you may be reunited can cause your ex not to take the breakup seriously, and it's unfair to keep him hanging.

"I'm never going to want to speak with you again. Doesn't that matter to you?" Don't panic or become consumed with guilt (even if you fear that you must have handled things badly). Do let your ex know, however, that he does matter to you. Often people say things like this to see if the other person cares enough to fight back. Showing that you care may help his bruised ego and sagging spirits.

Questions you'd rather not answer are difficult to hear. Since you can't stop someone from speaking their mind, you might as well try and find a way to speak yours—gently and carefully.

The Last Time a Guy Told Me He Wanted to Break Up I Went to Pieces. I Was So Surprised That I Handled It All Wrong. How Can I Handle Myself Better if it Happens Again?

Carol's Story

Michael and I got involved very quickly. We were crazy about each other. But after about two months Michael began to act very distant. I couldn't figure out what was happening. I thought it was his mood. One evening, after seeing a very romantic film, Michael said to me, "I don't feel the same about you." I was so shocked that I began sobbing. After a few minutes, Michael continued, "I think we should break up."

Sometimes I wonder if Michael would have broken up with me if I hadn't gotten hysterical.

It is *absolutely* possible to cause a breakup to be even messier, more painful and infinitely more regrettable for yourself and your boyfriend than it need be. Breakups are sometimes real shockers. Frustrations over missed signals and misinterpreted signs, plus the fear of being alone, can all add up to panic when a sudden separation leaps into the scene.

LOVE CYCLES

When someone you're involved with decides it's over, it's easy to feel victimized. You have to go along with something that you didn't want to happen. Your immediate reaction may be to say things you really don't mean. It's good to express your feelings, but first take the time to think about what you are saying. Doing so will help you avoid saying things you may later regret. Here are some tips on how to handle breaking up.

If he tells you it's over because he's feeling restless and wants to try new relationships:

- *Don't* ask him if he's met someone else he likes. He probably won't tell you, and there's no point in your knowing it right now anyway.
- *Don't* suggest seeing him less often on a more casual basis. Seeing an ex soon after a breakup can be painful. Why cause yourself more pain? Give yourself time to heal and then see what you want to do.
- *Don't* just get up and walk away. It's unfair to both of you. It's important to try and reach an understanding about the separation and each other's feelings. Only then will you be able to have nice, warm feelings about each other later on.

- *Do* ask him to explain how he's feeling. If he sees that you're not going to be on the attack, you may hear something that makes the entire situation less painful and more understandable. Affectionate words at this time can make the breakup more tolerable.
- *Do* take your time. When you sense your relationship is in trouble, take time to think. Emotional conversations can easily get away from you if you are not in touch with your feelings. Speaking before you know what you really want to say can be damaging.

If someone tells you he's interested in another girl:

- *Don't* ask him who she is and what she looks like. Comparing yourself to this girl will make you feel inadequate. It's not that this girl is any better than you but, because she has gained the attention of your boyfriend, you will naturally think she has something that you don't.
- *Don't* offer to keep seeing him while he explores a dating relationship with this other girl. You will undoubtedly feel jealous and threatened knowing your boy-

friend is dating another girl. Chances are you'll start looking for reassurance in all of his actions and if you don't find it, you'll feel let down. This kind of relationship can leave you feeling depressed and insecure and cause you to behave in ways unlike yourself.
- *Do*, if you feel your partner has been dishonest with you, tell him and give him a chance to explain. If he has gone behind your back, let him know you feel hurt and angry. If he lied with good reason, perhaps you should look into the way you've handled the relationship and see what you did that made him fearful of telling you the truth.

If he tells you his feelings have changed and he doesn't feel as strongly as he used to:

- *Don't* ask him what he doesn't like about you. If you carefully review your relationship, chances are you'll be able to understand why things didn't work out.
- *Don't* ask him to give it more time. People want out of a relationship often to get rid of pressure. A suggestion like this is simply *more* pressure.

- *Don't* ask him if he thinks he'll change his mind. Even if he suspects the answer may be "yes," he'll probably say "no" so that he doesn't have to feel you're waiting around for him.
- *Do* try and sort out what went on in the relationship that caused him to feel sour about it. (Don't blame yourself, as though it was *you* who made his feelings change.) Ask him if something happened that made him feel differently towards the relationship. By learning more about his feelings in connection with your relationship, you can determine whether any of this is a big misunderstanding, how much each of you contributed to the relationship's problems, and the best way to proceed from there.
- *Do* let him know you feel badly, and try suggesting that you not speak to each other for a while, or that you speak again when you feel a little calmer. He should know he's hit you with something very tough to hear. You have a right to pull yourself together before you give him any feedback.

Breakups are complicated and usually stem from *good* and *bad* feelings. People often need to make extreme statements about confusing is-

LOVE CYCLES

sues in order to make sense out of them. Don't get hung up over words or reasons. Try and understand his feelings, not for his sake but for yours, and then give *your* feelings a chance to become clear to you.

Once your feelings have settled, you will find it easier to express yourself, and the things you will be saying are those you mean to say!

Is There Such a Thing as a Good Time and Place to Break Up?

David's Story

Sue and I were not getting along anymore. I intended to discuss breaking up with her on our date last Saturday night, but we ended up at a party. I wanted to talk to her alone, but the walk home didn't seem to be the right time either.

The next day we went to a hockey game together and out for pizza afterward. The whole day there never seemed to be a good time to talk about our relationship because it was always so noisy.

I almost brought it up when we were sitting

under a tree in front of school on Tuesday, but I didn't want to upset her (or me) before a test.

Finally it occurred to me that all this waiting around for the "right" time was silly. I realized I'd just have to try and find *the time . . .*

There's no such thing as a good time and place to break up, but there certainly are better moments or environments to choose when discussing a breakup. An atmosphere that provides privacy for instance, is best, because it offers a place where you or your partner can be emotional and share open conversation.

To find the best conditions, all you really need is sensitivity and common sense. Here are some general guidelines that could help you find the time and place to make breaking up a bit more manageable:

- *Don't* break up if you know your boyfriend is having a tough problem at home or at school which you feel won't last very long. It might be better to wait for happier times before you tell him it's over. One, it would be very unfeeling to add to whatever suffering is already going on, and two, his present state of mind will probably make the upsetting confrontation even more difficult. (If you sense, however, that his is an ongoing problem, you may have to feel your way along until a moment arrives that seems reasonable enough.)

- *Don't* break up out of anger. Sometimes, a person you're close to can make you so hurt and furious that all you can think of doing is turning your back. Nothing *ever* gets settled this way and, in fact, things can turn rather ugly. Fury at a person you really care for is an indication of how much you care, not of how necessary it is for you to break up. True, to some extent it depends on the wrong that has been done to you, but for the most part both of you would profit far more from a heated serious discussion than a sudden breakup.
- *Don't* break up at parties or dances. Meaningful conversation, quiet tears and a few angry words are not things that ought to be witnessed by a crowd. Onlookers will inhibit your honest expression of feelings, and possibly add embarrassment to the already long list of uncomfortable feelings that are present in a breakup. Besides, why should anyone know your business before you've had a chance to let it sink in yourself?
- *Don't* break up right before a "special" date. Birthdays, Christmas parties, prom

nights and New Year's Eves are just a few examples of times you might want to let pass before separating. Breaking up brings lonely feelings with it, no matter when you decide to let it happen. Holidays and other celebratory occasions can make the emptiness feel that much worse. After all, you're *supposed* to feel so *wonderful* then! True, if the relationship isn't doing well, these special occasions may not be filled with fabulous moments anyway, but they might feel even more difficult if you strike out on your own at a time when most people (including yourself) are particularly in need of close company.

- *Don't* break up at a nice restaurant where you plan to have dinner. Even if you don't know the people around you, it can be very embarrassing to express your feelings in public and very difficult to hold them in as well. It's easy to feel trapped in a restaurant. Breakups are unpredictable. You may want to drag it out, cut it short, raise your voice, cry a little, or walk away for a minute. Restaurants are busy public places that offer endless possibilities for interruption. Why make the situation more difficult than it already is?
- *Do* try and arrange a conversation at a quiet out-of-the-way little cafeteria or cof-

fee shop. Pay for your sodas ahead of time, sit down and talk without fear of a waiter's interference. You might want to select a place that is *not* frequented by your friends. It could feel quite awkward if someone you knew walked in.
- *Do* suggest taking a walk in a neighborhood, perhaps familiar to you, but not your own. This way you'll avoid running into friends, but will still have the comfort of knowing your way around. Breaking up in a "foreign" place can make you feel even more lost and empty.
- *Do* take advantage of forced separations. If you know you and your boyfriend are going to be apart for a vacation or summer, wait before you break up. Use those weeks as a time for "seeing how you both feel." However, it is important to have an honest discussion about each other's expectations, so that no one returns home to a real shocker. It's good to think things through, explore other relationships free of guilt and get a handle on whatever pain and sadness both of you may be feeling. Time spent alone may even set the stage for a reconciliation!

There is never a good time to break up. There are simply times that are more appropriate than others. Look for them. Every little bit helps.

Most how-to guides are written with the intent of giving you all the advice and tools you need to make a difficult task easier. This chapter cannot do this because, unlike putting up wallpaper, fixing a car or building a bookshelf, this task is composed of too many unknowns.

These guidelines can't advise you on everything, because human emotions are too variable and unpredictable and unique. For every combination of personalities, emotions and situations, there are several ways to go—*anyone* would be hard-pressed to judge which route is the best.

But one thing this chapter can do is encourage you to think as clearly as you can about the situation at hand and the people involved. The ability to see your boyfriend as a *person*, no matter who is breaking up with whom, is crucial.

❤ STEP 5 ❤
Sticky Breakup Situations

Every breakup is unique. This is because no two people are alike, nor are the courses of any two relationships. Consider these breakup scenarios. The options and consequences are plentiful . . . but it's up to you to decide what would feel right for you.

You've recently broken up with a guy you cared a lot about. At first, the relationship had been wonderful. You couldn't have imagined anything better. After a while, however, things began to turn a little sour. Neither one of you seemed to understand the other's feelings, and you often walked away from a conversation unsatisfied. The relationship dragged on for a while as each of you were unwilling to admit that you didn't seem to be hitting it off anymore. Besides, there was one thing that was still feeling good—the physical closeness. Kissing and hugging was exciting.

Now the problem is, you've broken up with him but you're still physically attracted to him. Every time you see him you are very uncomfortable. Should you try and get the relationship back?

Some physical attractions stem from feeling close to someone. These linger on as long as your warm feelings for the person do. But other physical attractions come more from an immediate response to the way someone looks, moves, and/or smiles. This kind of attraction is often hard to shake, no matter how you feel about the person, as it stems from things somewhat unrelated to who the person really is. And there is an added difficulty if you've shared a pleasurable physical closeness. Shaking a pleasant memory connected with your attraction to someone is a very tough thing to do.

So don't spend so much time *trying!* The more you attempt to ignore it, or push it away, the more you may end up thinking about it!

You may want to try another tack instead: each time you see him, and are reminded of what it was like to kiss him, allow yourself to reflect on it for a moment. Don't fight it! Otherwise it will turn into something wonderfully forbidden! Then, think about something from the part of your relationship that was troublesome. Doing this will probably stir up some not-so-pleasant feelings and you may be surprised how easily you will be able to place those affectionate moments into perspective. You don't really want to simply *forget* the nice things, but you will want to find a way to keep them in their place.

It's very natural to still have all kinds of lingering feelings for a former boyfriend. For you right now, it's the physical closeness you miss. With another boyfriend in the future, you may miss the laughter, or the long serious talks. It's not realistic to expect you will be able to totally shut away everything that was good between you when it's all over. So the best thing to do is to try and temper your memories with some of the less attractive aspects of your relationship. It should help you achieve a nice balance.

There's one other reason to keep what was good in perspective! The tendency to exaggerate the good points of an ex when he's floating around in your memory can make it impossible for a new guy to *ever* measure up!

• • •

You've recently decided to break up with a guy you'd been seeing for a few months. You had slowly come to believe that he just wasn't right for you and, to make matters worse, you had been getting the disquieting feeling that he was much too dependent on you. It seemed best to end the relationship before things got out of hand, and so you did, in what turned out to be one brief conversation. He was so upset he could barely listen, and you were so distressed you could hardly speak.

But now, a month later, he has started sending you notes . . . notes that express his affection, sense of loss and hope for the relationship he's sure the two of you still can have together. So far you haven't answered the letters, but you know you'll have to do something at some point. You just don't know what.

Just because a relationship is over, in the sense that one person has told the other that it cannot continue, *does not mean* that both people involved can be expected to cleanly "make a break." Fortunately, and unfortunately, emotions don't work that way, and these lingering feelings could mean any number of things.

They could indicate simply that a strong affection still exists. (Which does not necessarily mean you should get back together; love can hang around even when incompatibility takes over.) They could mean the breakup is stirring

LOVE CYCLES

up bad memories relating to other romances or personal problems. Their presence could also be due to insecurities, *or* the fact that a person feels there's some unfinished business—that there are things which need to be talked out. The reasons can be as complicated as love itself.

Whatever the cause, however, this inability to "let go" is a terribly painful problem, and to some degree it should not be made to rest entirely on one person's shoulders. After all, it did take *two* people to get involved. While certainly you cannot blame yourself for your ex's inability to forget the romance, you can try to help him reach an understanding of why you feel things must come to an end. By doing so, you might even clear up a few unanswered questions for yourself, especially since the last conversation you had was hardly a satisfying one!

Reaching out in some way towards your ex can be a good idea. But you, of course, have your own feelings to contend with and protect. Think carefully about what you would be most comfortable doing and then proceed.

- You could call and, after expressing your good feelings for him, also communicate your confusion over his letters. Tell him honestly but tactfully how you feel about your relationship, letting him know you're uncomfortable with what his letters seem to imply. In other words, let him know that you're prepared to listen to him, you care enough about him to respond, but you're not prepared to change your decision. If he chooses to express his hurt feelings, let him. But if you begin to sense that the conversation is getting out of control and that his feelings are truly upsetting you, gently bow out of the conversation by saying you hope things go well for him but right now you really must have some space. You owe him your ear, not your soul.

- Another, perhaps less risky, move would be to write him a letter. In this way you could maintain some control through distance, and give yourself the opportunity to clearly express both your positive and negative feelings. It is possible that a well thought out and caring response could have a soothing effect and lead to a resolution more quickly.

When there are troubles in your relationship, you are in a rough position—there is no denying that. You have your own emotions to deal with, and on top of that, your boyfriend may be asking you to help him deal with his hurt and confusion. If such is the case, the best thing you can do is to listen and respond as caringly as you are able to without compromising your position. If you think it's over, then that's what you think. If you feel sad but not torn by your decision, then that's what you feel. And if he can't accept your feelings, once you've taken a bit more time to look at them with him, then that is not your fault.

If his disquieting behavior persists, you may either have to ignore it, tell him you simply cannot handle it any longer, or suggest that he confide his emotions in someone else. It is for you to be reasonably concerned, but it's not for you to suffer.

Note: Making a date to see him for this discussion is not presented as an option, largely because it could open you up for a very difficult emotional confrontation—one that would be hard to walk away from. A phone call or a letter would provide you with a chance to feel out of the situation. If after that you feel it would be good to see each other, then go ahead! Having some idea of what you can expect could make all of the difference!

A few weeks ago you began to feel restless and uninterested in your boyfriend. You'd been going with him for about four months and for a while things had been very good. But now, you find your mind is constantly wandering when you are with him, and even though you still like him very much, it seems to you that there might be someone else out there.

So you break up and promptly begin looking around.

That weekend you're invited to a party. You go alone and run straight into your ex who is accompanied by another girl. You take one good long look at him and suddenly realize that you wish you'd given the relationship another shot. Smiling warmly, you walk over and greet him enthusiastically, but after giving you a cool hello, he turns his back and walks away.

Under certain circumstances, the sound of a past love's voice or a glimpse of his or her face can be a very powerful and disconcerting thing. This confusion *could* mean a reconsideration of the breakup is in order, but it could also simply mean that the two of you still have tender feelings for each other . . . and that's all.

Therefore, it is terribly important for you to try and understand exactly what it was that inspired your sudden urge to resume the relationship with your ex; and to sort this out as best you can *before* you do anything about it! Acting without thinking could set you both up for unnecessary hurt.

To understand your feelings better, try asking yourself some questions. Had you been thinking about him a lot lately? Was there something about him that suddenly began to stand out for you, especially when you began dating other guys with whom you weren't impressed? Have you been lonely these last few weeks?

There is also the question of how much your immediate environment is affecting your emotions. Parties can be romantic and exciting or simple fun—or very lonely. If you're alone and a bit sad (or with a date you're not feeling good about) the sight of other couples can be hard to take. Not being a part of the romantic scene can make you feel lonely. Seeing your old boyfriend may cause you to think you want him back. But remember the situation you are in. If you were out to dinner with your family, would you still want him back? Maybe after breaking up it is best to avoid such trying environments and give yourself time to heal.

If you have reasonably considered your feelings and the situation, and have concluded your interest is sincere, then there are a few ways to go.

A couple of days after the party, try giving him a call. Although it may be difficult to resist, don't beat around the bush. Understandably, you might be interested first in finding out how involved he is with this new girl, but try to keep from bringing her up. After all it is *your* relationship that you're interested in, not theirs.

Let him know you've been having some regrets and tell him about the feelings that overcame you at the party. He will feel complimented but probably confused, since it was you who left him. In expressing your positive feelings, try to communicate caution—for both your sakes. Saying you want to be a couple again, "right now, no doubt about it," could put terrible pressure on both of you. You'll feel worse if it doesn't work, and he may begin to feel that somehow this second time he's really "failed" or been "tricked." Suggest that you miss him and would like to start seeing him again, but in a way that would involve minimal strain and lots of growing room.

The other option you have is to call him and, instead of talking about it right then and there, set up a date to discuss both yours and his feelings in person. But be aware that you could be creating a very awkward scene. He may prefer the safety of a phone call to an out-and-out confrontation and, in the end, so might you.

Personal encounters are usually much more emotional and more difficult to control. Tension, hurt and anxiety are deep-rooted feelings that are hard to experience and express at the same time. The intensity of your emotions is something to consider before getting together. It's true, some people would rather have it out right in the open, finding the phone too impersonal. But for some, that "impersonal" quality makes an extremely personal problem easier to face.

As for the response he gives you, you'll have to prepare yourself ahead of time for absolutely anything. Don't kid yourself about that. He may be furious, he may jump at the chance to get back together, he may tell you he's developing strong feelings for this other girl, or he may tell you he needs time to think. You will just have to respect and accept his decision. Remember, you're asking him to take another chance in an arena in which he already got hurt. It's understandable he may be hesitant about a reconciliation.

Lately it seems your boyfriend has been acting especially irritable when the two of you are together. It almost feels as though he's looking for a fight—trying to find things that bother him so that the two of you will get into an argument. It's taken all you've got to keep from losing your temper and you're nearing the end of your rope. You have a strong sense that what he really wants is to break up, but you're so angry and confused that you don't want to give in to it.

If your instincts tell you there's *big* trouble ahead, but your boyfriend won't admit to anything being wrong, it's no surprise that you might want to close your eyes to what's going on and hope the storm blows over.

The problem with this is that, if you fail to prepare yourself to meet what could merely be a summer shower, you might end up the victim of a tornado. If indeed your boyfriend is trying to tell you something, it's a good idea to find out what it is. Don't let obvious signals go unnoticed. Ignoring a problem won't make it go away, and could possibly make it worse. If the air needs to be cleared and no one takes the initiative to talk about what's going on, tension will result. Lingering tension within a relationship can cause it to fall apart.

Of course, you don't want to go asking for trouble either. There's always the possibility that you are feeling very sensitive and misinterpreting your boyfriend's actions. In all fairness to both of you, it might be better to investigate the problem in a way that gently opens the door for conversation—as opposed to abruptly flinging it open, poised for "round one."

Try telling him that you feel as though he's been behaving a little short-tempered lately. Explain that you're not sure if you're reading him wrong, but is there something bothering him? Be sure to make it clear that you're *not* criticizing him. You're just trying to see what's going on. After all, why should you give him reason

LOVE CYCLES

to behave defensively, when what you really need is for him to speak honestly?

Another approach might be to let him know you've been feeling uncomfortable with him lately and that it seems to you he's always upset or angry when you're together. Ask him if he'd like to talk about it because you'd rather try and understand what's going on instead of just sitting around feeling anxious and unhappy.

You might want to let it go until the next time he blows his cool and then take the opportunity, after you've sorted out the problem at hand, to ask him if he's noticed these kinds of arguments have been cropping up a lot lately. Does he have any idea why?

All of these approaches should "gently" do the trick. Don't accuse him angrily of being difficult. Instead, express your distress over his troublesome behavior and your willingness to hear him out. Your goal is to get him to speak about what may be wrong by gently stating your observations instead of blowing up and inspiring an angry confrontation the two of you may later regret.

As for what you'll hear in response to your comments, it's impossible to predict. You could find yourself anywhere from tremendously relieved—because all along it was a problem that had nothing to do with you—or in the first stage of a breakup. But whether this conversation finds you two closer than ever or on the way to a split, it's worth having. Chances are the trouble you face will be a lot simpler than the mess you may create by avoiding a confrontation.

Two nights ago you broke up with your boyfriend. It was a long emotional evening in which you tried your best to explain how you felt (though it was difficult since you weren't all that clear on it yourself!). When your conversation with him drew to a close, you had the distinct feeling that your boyfriend was still terribly confused and hurt, and all in all you weren't feeling very well either. You still care about him, but you know deep down inside that it was time to move on.

Suddenly, this morning, you received an agitated phone call from him. He just remembered the silver bracelet he gave you for your birthday, and he wants it back. It was a meaningful and touching gift for you, and the thought of giving it up hurts.

Gifts that are exchanged as expressions of affection usually become cherished belongings. They come to represent everything that was warm, giving and loving in a relationship both for the giver and the receiver, and thus can be very powerful symbols.

It's little wonder each of you are experiencing conflicting emotions over the bracelet. For you it embodies the warm and lovely romantic moments you shared with your ex . . . moments you'd love to hang on to in some way. For him, the bracelet represents his affection, which you have now turned away. His asking for the return of the gift may be a way of saying, "If you don't want me, give back every piece of me."

But there's something else he might be asking for, too. He may be trying to find out if you still care for him and if *he* can hurt you as you have him. It's also possible that the request for the bracelet is a hefty combination of both motivations.

There are a few ways to go. Whose hand the bracelet eventually rests in will depend solely on the small dynamic and emotional qualities each of you bring to this confrontation.

- You could refuse to return the bracelet. It *is* yours, it was not given to you in return for your promise to date him forever. You could explain that you want to keep the bracelet because it symbolizes to you all the wonderful times you shared together.
- You could give it back without an argument, but with a gentle unhappy manner. Handing it back would be a sign that you are willing to do as he asks. Perhaps you could take this opportunity to try and talk

him out of it by explaining that the gift is meaningful to you and that it would mean a lot to you to keep it.
- You could tell him right up front that you don't want to give it back, explain your feelings, and ask him to think about it for a while. Tell him you *will* return it if you must, but that you would like to keep it because it holds warm memories of a special time in your life. This may give him a chance to cool off, but it may also make him even angrier because you are arguing with him.
- You could go up to your room, letting your anger rule, bring the bracelet down to the door and place it self-righteously in his hand when he appears. With an expression on your face that reads, "You want it? It's fine with me!" you could then swiftly close the door. If, in fact, one of the problems in your relationship was his need to "get back," perhaps for you this demand of his is the last straw. Behaving as angrily and resentfully as you may feel could be just what he had coming.

In all probability, this request for the bracelet originated from a mixture of sadness, anger, hurt and resentment. Undoubtedly, your reaction to the request will be influenced by a similar set of emotions. How you decide to behave will be affected by the particulars of your past and present relationship with your ex. The degree of patience, understanding or anger you bring to the situation will naturally be somewhat dependent on how you've felt over the last few weeks. If you've been in a fury, this request will further infuriate you. If you've been depressed, his desire may further sadden you. If you're tremendously relieved over having made a decision and acted on it, you may feel less inclined to fight over the romantic trinket.

But the most important thing to keep in mind is that there's probably more to his request than meets the eye. It would be a good idea to try to look past his words, his state of mind and your own emotions to establish a communication which will give each of you a chance to come away with something you both need.

♥ PART III ♥

RECOVERY AND DISCOVERY!

❤ STEP 6 ❤
Feeling Rotten

Lisa and Michael had been seeing each other for about six months when things started getting rocky. At first it was only small arguments over silly little issues such as who pays for the sodas. But suddenly, these minor tiffs began to blossom into larger conflicts such as each of their rights to go out with a friend on Friday night instead of with each other.

At first they tried to avoid a big confrontation over the problem, fearing it would end their relationship. Eventually, though, it became clear that the two of them would have to face each other. One night over a soda Lisa and Michael began a discussion about their relationship, and two hours later realized they had differences they couldn't resolve. Their definitions as to what makes a *good* boyfriend or girlfriend just didn't seem to match. Sadly the two of them decided to call it quits.

Now, weeks later, Lisa is still uninterested in anyone else, feeling a bit dragged down, and generally fearful over her own inability to put the entire relationship behind her.

The aftermath of a breakup is sometimes very rough. How could it not be? But part of getting over a relationship is weathering this rough period. In fact, it's actually important to leave room for hurt and difficult feelings, for it's the first step in getting over them! They are significant emotions from which you can learn a lot about your relationships, yourself, and the ways in which you can get over a breakup and move on. If you were to turn your back completely on these feelings, you might find yourself a part of the mainstream once again, but you would also be cheating yourself out of a very valuable learning experience. By allowing yourself to feel the full range of your emotions, you will better understand how you feel about what has happened. In the end, you will feel resolved and more prepared if you should have to face a similar encounter in the future.

Finding love is one of the most glorious experiences anyone could ever have. Losing it is considered by many to be the worst. . . . But, just as you have to move through a love relationship before a loss can occur, so you must move through the loss to find another love.

I Can't Seem to Get Over a Breakup That Happened Two Weeks Ago. We'd Been Pretty Close, So I Guess I Miss Him, Even Though I Know We're Probably Not Right for Each Other. But Lately I Feel Empty and Lonely. What's Going On?

There are a number of things that are "going on" which are difficult to pinpoint and even harder to label. They are emotions that almost everyone feels to greater or lesser degrees, no matter where they stand in the breakup.

Loss

Let's face it. You've lost something! There *is* no getting around that. There was an important person in your life who filled a significant slot in your personal social needs. He received the affections you love to give and he gave you the affections you love to receive. The giving and taking of romantic love and affection is fundamental to most people's happiness. Thus, when it suddenly disappears, it's no wonder you feel a sense of emptiness. It takes time to adjust to not having someone to share physical and emotional closeness.

But it's also important to see that, contrary to what the word "loss" connotes, not all losses are negative ones. It's true that if you lose something you are minus that thing, but sometimes you have to let things go in order to gain something in their place. This notion of replacement won't lessen the pain of the loss, but it should help you see that, when it's over, you will move forward. You will learn from your past experience and be able to use this newly found knowledge to better your next relationship.

Disappointment

Disappointment over a relationship gone sour is common and usually appears for a number of unfortunate reasons.

Most of the time we enter into a relationship we do so with high hopes and passionate dreams—"This one will be true love," we tell ourselves. But this infatuation with a partner usually wears off as the two people get to know each other better. Infatuation has a dreamlike quality in that it is full of fantasies of what you hope to gain from your relationship. Once the relationship becomes more established, what you can expect from your partner becomes more clearly defined. Dreams give way to reality, and sometimes the reality is just too far away from the dream to be accepted. Thus disappointment sets in.

It is common to feel disappointment in yourself. The fantasy is often, "There must have been something I could have said or done to save our romance." But this just isn't so. You cannot single-handedly manage or manipulate a relationship. There's another thinking, feeling person in the couple with you who is going to follow his needs, often regardless of your own. As the expression goes, "It takes two to tango," and it takes two to make a relationship work.

Disappointment isn't fun. But sometimes it's a lot better to experience the sadness that comes with it than the confusion and inevitable hurt that happens when one doesn't face the truth.

Embarrassment

Evy's Story

Peter and I had been an item for weeks. It was so much fun! But Christmas vacation Peter went away to Florida with his parents, and when he got back he announced that he wanted to break up. He said he wanted the freedom to see other people. I was positive he had met someone new, but he insisted he hadn't. He just realized he was feeling trapped. It had nothing to do with other girls or me.

Of course I didn't believe him. I was sure it was all me. I was so sure that I didn't want to face my friends. I even started having bad dreams about it. But a few weeks later this cute guy sat down next to me on the school steps. We started talking (I still felt so embarrassed because I just knew he knew!), and he asked me out! I suddenly realized that I was the only one who saw myself as a loser!

Unfortunately, people often assume that, if a relationship falls apart, *somebody did* something wrong. The person who is broken up with feels that he or she is not good enough to keep their partner interested in the relationship.

Let's face it. If you're going to think this

way, it may take you *years* to get over the embarrassment. Of course it can be embarrassing if someone breaks up with you and everyone knows that you still want the relationship. But, ultimately, everyone finds themselves in this position at some point or other. It is the natural way of relationships.

Try to remember, when embarrassment threatens to overwhelm you, that the ability to be in a relationship at all is something to be proud of. It takes a lot of maturity to be able to give and take and care in a way that keeps you and another person happy—even if it is for a shorter time than you would like.

So think about that a little when you feel that you can't show your face! There are a lot of people out there who are too afraid to even *try* a relationship. You've got guts!

Rejection

When someone breaks up with you, rejection is the hardest emotion to handle. First of all, you still have feelings for your ex and probably would like to get back together. This longing for your boyfriend may make you feel depressed and lonely, and terribly critical of yourself. You may begin to evaluate your shortcomings and eventually allow them to grow larger than your attributes. Finally you may put two and two together and simply decide you are unlovable.

Don't do it. It's all too easy to blow everything out of proportion when rejection hits. Of course it's good to examine what you may have done that contributed negatively to your relationship. But obviously you have something good to offer since your ex was attracted to you in the first place.

To understand rejection, you must understand that people leave others *far* more frequently because of the changing needs, problems and desires *they* have. It isn't simply due to what their partner lacks. It's true that you may not fit their ideas of what they now need, but try and look at it this way: Why should you fit their image? You'll be changing too, in your own special way. That's what continues to make you interesting. If he feels that you're not right for him anymore, in truth, maybe you're not. But why does not being right for him have to automatically mean you're not right, period? The two of you may not be compatible right now. That much you must accept. That he realized a difference between you before you were ready to face it is painful, but it is also a truth you *must* deal with. Still, it's equally important to accept that you are not any less for having been left. In fact, in all probability as time goes on you may discover you are all the better for it!

And above all, remember that people often break up for reasons that are as unclear to the person who is leaving as they are to the one who is being left. So don't go overboard trying to understand his decision. Chances are you'll never get to the real reason for his breaking up. He may even have a fear of becoming too involved, in which case, feelings of rejection would be a torturous mistake!

Fear

Most people experience some degree of fear when they enter a relationship. There is the fear of rejection, embarrassment and, most of all, the fear of loss.

Upon experiencing a breakup, you may fear what others think, what's "wrong" with you, what your ex must be feeling about you—and you're bound to worry about where your next date will come from, being alone, your attractiveness, why you *really* wanted to end the relationship, why he *really* wanted to end the relationship, etc., etc.

All of these fears and worries are normal and

often difficult to overcome. Much of how you handle your fears will really depend on how deep they run and how you feel about yourself to begin with. For the most part, fears can't be taken away from you. You have to place yourself in situations that challenge them. One of the biggest reasons this is so tough to do is that our imagination can make any predicament far worse than it really is.

Sitting alone in your room, you imagine that your ex thinks you're awful, your friends are laughing, and every potential date is writing you *out* of his book. But open your door and chances are you'll discover your ex has been feeling a bit mopey himself, your friends all miss you, and there's a guy out there who's been *waiting* for you to break up so that he can make his move.

Hiding can make you not only *look* afraid, guilty and depressed, but also *feel* that way. If you feel that way people will see it in you. So what's the sense of making yourself miserable? Go out with your friends and try to have some fun. You'll see that life isn't as dismal as it seemed when you were sitting alone in your room. Your friends will see the change in your mood, and knowing they sense this about you will help boost your confidence.

Now That I Have an Idea of Why I'm Feeling the Way I Am, How Can I Get Through This Time? It Can Be So Unbearable!

Jimmy's Story

I was aching like crazy after Lynn and I broke up. I didn't think I'd be able to stand it, and I wasn't talking to anyone about it. Finally, my older sister came home from college for vacation, and one night I told her about how I was feeling. It felt so good to let it out that I couldn't seem to stop talking. I even told her the color of Lynn's sweater the night we broke up.

When I got into bed that night, I still felt sad, but something was different. I felt a little lighter . . . as if someone had taken a big burden off my shoulders.

The next day I was able to concentrate in class for the first time in weeks . . .

There are many ways to go about handling a breakup. Think your options over carefully, because your choice can mean the difference between feeling better or aggravating the situation and causing you a lot of grief.

- *Don't* call your ex to comfort you. If you broke up with him, it would be a selfish move. If he broke up with you, it could prove to be a very self-destructive decision. Chances are he would have nothing new to say that would really, in a meaningful way, help you out. You might even be opening yourself up for another hurtful confrontation.
- *Don't* spend all of your time searching for the "real" answer and reasons for your broken romance. A little time spent on the subject is necessary and inevitable, but *constant* attention to your ex and the relationship will not do a thing for you except drive you up the wall! Reasons are never black and white. You could think and question forever and never *really* know what happened.
- *Don't* torture yourself with romantic movies or novels. Sometimes it feels good to have a good cry, and if you need to watch a moving romantic film to allow yourself the freedom, then go ahead. But don't make it a habit!
- *Don't* fill your head with bigger-than-life negative thoughts like: 1) I'll never meet another person like him; 2) He's the best I'll ever get; 3) I'll never fall in love

again or 4) I hope I didn't make the biggest mistake of my life.
- *Do* realize that: 1) you may not meet another person like him, but you'll meet someone who has other wonderful things to offer. 2) People cannot be judged as good, very good or best ever. They are only as great or as terrible as what *we* see in them. When you're ready to see how terrific someone can be, and a good candidate happens along—you'll have "the best" once again. 3) Falling in love is so special that when it happens it seems like it's never going to happen again—it's too much of a miracle. But love is not entirely a miracle. It's a wonderful thing that doesn't happen every day between people, but it usually happens more than once. This is not to take the magic away. This is just to say that love is a constant factor in life. It's not a one-time award. The only thing is, love *never* happens the *same* way twice, nor does it ever *feel* the exact same way. Still, it's fabulous and exciting *every* time! 4) As far as "mistakes" go, if you're right for each other and the timing is right, in all probability you'll find each other again. Forgiveness and apologies seem insignificant when love is at stake.

- *Do* call a good friend or speak to an older brother or sister. Express your pent-up emotions by allowing yourself the time and freedom to really talk to someone who cares. It's important to find an outlet for your unhappiness. The only way it will ever leave you is if you put it before you, look at it, feel it, and then allow it to fade away, as it surely will.
- *Do* accept dates with friends to go to movies and, *if* you're in the mood, parties. But don't feel obligated to push yourself into a crowded room. While parties are fun, there is usually romance in the air, which can make you feel uncomfortable if you're not ready for it. But don't avoid them for too long! A brief vacation from the social scene is a reasonable response to a break up; however, an entire semester's worth is *not!*
- *Do* take yourself to comedic films and perhaps the mystery/thriller shelves of your bookstore. Call a friend, turn on the TV, or go out and do something physical. Believe it or not, most sports can freshen up your entire outlook. Try it!

After a breakup, no matter who is responsible, both people usually go through a period of confusion, discomfort and sadness. The reason it is so hard to sort these feelings out is that it's not just one emotion that inspires this difficult time, but rather a mixture of many.

Clearly, to some degree all of these emotions are unavoidable, understandable reactions. You cannot just make them disappear. But the extent to which you get carried away by false, painful assumptions about yourself and the meaning of the breakup is something you can control. Understanding where the truth stops and all of your worst insecurities take over will help you to gain a more realistic perspective of the situation and deal with it accordingly.

It's important to let yourself feel whatever it is that comes along and to not let it scare you or overwhelm you to the point that you do things that make it worse.

These rotten feelings are natural, but they aren't permanent. Just how temporary they are depends on you!

❤ STEP 7 ❤

Being On Your Own

Things had not been going well for Pam and her boyfriend Paul for some time. It's hard to remember when the real trouble started, but she hadn't felt close to him ever since that evening the two of them got into an argument over her unaffectionate mood. She explained that there'd been some trouble at home and she was feeling upset. Paul had never been a particularly understanding guy (at least in terms of Pam's mood swings) and that night was no exception. It seemed that ever since then, things had gone from pretty bad to pretty terrible.

They stayed together, however, and last night was the big dance. The two of them had made plans to go with three other couples. Pam was all dressed up and flushed with excitement, anticipating the evening ahead. On the dance floor, the romantic couples whirled around gracefully, but as she turned to Paul with a smile on her lips her heart sank.

She felt nothing. Pam tried to convince herself that at least she had a date for the dance and a sure Saturday evening partner. Didn't that make it worth it?

Close romantic companionship is a wonderful thing. Everyone needs it, everyone can learn a great deal from it, and everyone will know few joys that are greater than falling in love.

But it is not something that can or should be attained at *any* price. Though love is important for *everyone*, it is not *everything*. Neither "true love" nor a "steady date" will ever be the fulfilling experience it could be if the people involved are not there for the right reasons. Fear of being alone is definitely not a good reason to become involved, nor is it realistic. And there's a reason for this.

When you are no longer seeing someone, you are *not* alone. You are simply *on your own*. Most people do not see this crucial difference, and so the fear takes over.

Fear of "being alone" can lead people to stay in relationships that are no longer working;

build relationships on a damaging amount of dependence; cause people to turn away from arguments that need to be argued; and ignore hurts that need to be resolved. Furthermore, it can stop people from taking important opportunities which lie before them, as they are too afraid of leaving the familiar and reaching for the unknown.

No relationship can ever *really* work unless the people involved are together *not* because they fear being alone, but because they love and respect each other. Only in this kind of genuine relationship will each person feel free to express what's really at their very core—and have the courage to be themselves.

Romance can satisfy many of your social needs. You no longer have to make phone calls and plans to fill your social calendar. It is taken for granted that much of your free time will be spent with your boyfriend. But once the romance ends, and if you give yourself a chance, you will find there are terrific alternatives. You may have to apologize to friends if you've been out of touch but, once all is forgiven and friendships are re-established, you'll see that being without romance is nothing to fear. And hopefully you'll learn a valuable lesson in the interim—friendships are just as important as romance. In fact, they can even enhance your next relationship.

I Don't See How Being on My Own Is an Experience That Will Help My Future Romances.

Being free gives you an important sense of confidence and self-reliance. The "you" you bring to this new romance will be someone who is there because she wants to be, *not* because she needs to be.

Having had time to develop all kinds of interests and nurture friendships, your romance will not be your entire life. You will make time for your boyfriend and likewise make time in your romance for your favorite sport or hobby. The freedom to take time for yourself to pursue personal interests will make the time spent together fresh and appreciated. You will have new and different things to talk about and grow from. Besides, since a relationship shouldn't be everything in life, this openness will allow you both to explore all life has to offer and keep you from becoming too dependent on each other—a perfect arrangement!

Heightened confidence in yourself and your ability to manage on your own will help you confront problems in your relationship. You will no longer overlook those things that bother you because you will no longer fear breaking up. Let's face it, if your relationship is not making you happy, then it's not worth having. If you are able to face the problems head-on, without the burden of feeling terrified of aloneness and helplessness, getting past the rocky times will be easier and clearer.

Relationships need to be open-ended, constantly ready to welcome new ideas, activities and experiences. If both people are out there in the world, independently getting involved, seeing and feeling things, they will bring what they've discovered back to each other. Both people will try new things, venture into new interests and get to know new people. Without this constant filtering in of new experiences, a relationship can become stagnant. Two people can smother each other. If you're in the habit of exploring on your own, chances are you'll take this skill into the relationship. The two of you will thrive on it!

Being on your own before entering a new relationship can really help you see the value of being on your own *in* a relationship. It takes two separate people to make a successful couple. There are times when the two of you will *feel* like one, and such a sensation is truly wonderful. But in reality you will never be one. So you might as well be all that you can be on your own and let him find out just how wonderful you are!

My Fear of Being Alone Stops Me From Ending Relationships Which I Know Should End . . . and I'm Usually Miserable the Whole Time!

Priscilla's Story

I was miserable with Steve. All we were doing was fighting . . . or rather all I was doing was yelling while he turned a deaf ear. I knew we had to stop seeing each other, but I wanted him to make the first move.

I guess he was as scared as I was. I mean, who wants to be alone?

Finally, after a horrendous scene at a dance (where I started flirting with another guy and Steve hit the roof), we broke up. I was terrified . . . until I discovered the drama club.

The only thing I'm sorry about now is that Steve and I can't even be friends. The breakup was too ugly.

It is very understandable, once you are in the habit of "having" someone by your side, to feel afraid of striking out on your own. But again, it is important to remember that you are going to be *on your own* and *not alone*.

There *are* other people out there, and even if all of your girlfriends have a steady, there will be times when you can make arrangements to see them alone or with their boyfriends. It won't be easy, and their relationships might make you miss having one all the more, but there are people out there who will continue to care for you. If you allow them to give you comfort and companionship, you may discover that being on your own makes for an intense period of discovery. You may even find in your friends, and in yourself, qualities you never recognized before.

Here are some steps you can take to teach yourself how to feel good on your own:

- Tell your good friends what you are afraid of. Saying it will take away some of the sting and will afford them the opportunity to be supportive and comforting. Good friends will *not* leave you when you need someone to talk to. Besides, telling your friends what you fear may inspire them to find a date or two for you—a move they might not have made so quickly had you not expressed your distress over being alone.
- Recognize that, in addition to looking to your friends for support, you can look to yourself. There's a lot to you! Use it! Instead of dreading the extra time you may find on your hands, take advantage of it. Look into racquetball, jewelry mak-

ing or whatever activity has always attracted you. And don't be embarrassed that you need to fill your time with these things instead of romance. Pretty soon you could be enjoying yourself so much that you wouldn't give up your new interests for anyone (though you'd certainly alter your schedule just a bit!).

Whatever happens, don't let fear get the better of you. You'll have no idea what you're missing if you never really spend time with yourself and get to know who you are. Anyway, prolonging a very destructive relationship isn't a good alternative to making it on your own.

I'm Afraid of What Being Alone "Looks" Like. I Really Think People Will Wonder What's Wrong With Me.

Chances are people won't give much thought to your being unattached. Everybody goes through different relationships until they find the person they want to settle down with. Your in-between-romances stage is nothing unusual. But in order to let go of those terrible thoughts you fear others have about you, you must first get rid of the ones you fear about yourself. Only then will you be able to laugh at your own insecurities, the thoughts you think *they* have, and the negative thoughts (perhaps even insulting!) they may indeed harbor.

Compose a list of the things you fear other people are thinking and try to honestly figure out how much is really your own anxiety. Don't be alarmed if your list seems endless! It just means you're being very honest with yourself and that when you're down on yourself you have a very active imagination!

A Sample List:

I'm alone because . . .

- I'm not attractive to other guys.
- I can't keep a guy.
- I'm not attracted to guys.
- I'm not mature enough to have a meaningful relationship.
- I'm hard to get along with.
- As soon as someone gets to know the "real" me, they're no longer interested.

- I'm all show, no action.
- I'm afraid of sex, etc.

All of these fears are terribly painful, but probably also blown out of proportion. Sure, right now you may be so disgusted or hurt over a past relationship that you aren't attracted to other guys. Maybe you are a little moody and so it takes a tolerant person to really understand you. The prospects of physical intimacy might make you nervous and sometimes you may feel too eaten up by your own problems to really want to give to someone else. But the differences between these possibilities and the list of fears is *tremendous!*

It can be helpful to your own growth to recognize the speck of truth in each of these fears. Learning to understand why you feel the way you do about yourself can put your fears in their proper perspective. Too many times we attach labels to our emotions rather than take the time to work them through. You may find that this is true with some of the fears on your list.

As for what other people may think, people who look down on you without knowing the facts are usually insecure. They feel easily threatened by any changes they see going on around them. Often they put down your misfortune to make themselves feel better about their own predicament. Sometimes, seeing someone go through what they would consider a "bad" time makes them feel vulnerable. Also talking about the person in the bad situation allows people to express the fears they would have if it were happening to them.

So let people think what they want! If it's a good friend and you're a little paranoid about what he or she is thinking, there's nothing wrong with expressing your worst fears. In fact, it's sometimes a good way to get some badly needed reassurances. But if it's just a crowd of kids who you suspect are saying nasty things behind your back, give them the same mysterious smiles they give you.

They'll start to wonder what you have on them . . . and you'll have the satisfaction of knowing the answer. *Plenty!*

But Can I Ever Really Enjoy Being Alone? Life Is So Much Nicer When I Have Someone.

Life does seem fuller, more exciting and filled with warmth and security when you're involved in a romance. This does not, however, mean that life cannot still be full, exciting and oozing with warmth and security. It's just that you'll have to experience these good feelings with people other than a boyfriend.

Dating several guys without any romantic commitments can be *wonderful*. Seeing so many people attracted to you will feel exciting. Being cared for even without making a commitment will fill you with warmth. And having each of your dates expose you to their hobbies and interests will bring a new fullness to your life.

Spending time with good friends can be fabulously fulfilling. It takes a lot of time and sharing to build warm, understanding friendships that can last a lifetime. Often a relationship can inhibit you from making close friends because of its high demands on your time. But friendships are not things to be pushed aside. Sometimes, when a romance is over a circle of close friends can do wonders for your feelings of aloneness and rejection and can actually help you find ways to enjoy your new freedom.

Quiet times alone can be the key to your sense of self-reliance. Taking time for yourself gives you the freedom to develop new interests, read a good book, complete an entry in a diary or simply to ponder past relationships and experiences, current problems or new people in your life. Self-reflection can shed fresh light on old ideas, and help you find new ways to resolve old problems. Either way, you'll grow to understand yourself a little better.

What If I'm Dating Someone I Like, but I Don't Want a Commitment and He's Pushing Me to Get More Involved?

You can't make someone be patient if he doesn't want to be, but you can try to give him reasons for your wanting to slow it down. If you express yourself clearly and sensitively he will probably be willing to give your relationship some time.

Below are a few ways to approach the new guy you are seeing:

- "I still feel the need to be on my own, I just got over a heavy relationship and I don't want to rush into this one. I hope you understand because I really do like you."
- "Please don't push me. I have a good time with you, but when you push me to get closer I start feeling anxious. I guess

I need more time and I hope you'll decide to give it to me."
- "We get along so well and you really make me happy, but I'm just not ready to get more involved right now. I realize you don't have to wait around for me, and that you have to do what feels right for you. I hope we can keep seeing each other. I really do. But I'll understand if you decide against it."

When confronting your date, you first want to let him know that you care about him. Otherwise, he may think you're not interested in him. Don't harp on your past romance, it will only make your date feel rotten inside. It's painful to think that the person you really like used to be involved with someone else. Just be honest and make sure to express enthusiasm for the relationship, and things should work out fine!

Being on your own is an opportunity to explore your life—a life that, in the face of a major romance, is frequently neglected. It's sad but true that friends, interests and even yourself can go unattended when there's a romance afoot. This kind of single-mindedness rarely does anything positive for a relationship.

Still, people fear independence, and despite the knowledge that dependence can be destructive, they will opt for a relationship even if it means having no life of their own. But not every relationship has to be smothering. After all, romance enhances life in a special way. But however wonderful the relationship may be, romance does not *make* life. So, whether you're in a relationship or on your own, take advantage of spending time with yourself. You'll learn what a terrific person you are and, as a result, build a relationship that sincerely respects your individuality. After all, *first* you're a person, *then* you're a couple!

❤ STEP 8 ❤
Full Circle: A Fresh Beginning

It's been about a month since Lisa and Mark's breakup. Lisa has spent a lot of time thinking about the good times, looking at souvenirs from special nights and generally reliving the moments that were particularly meaningful to her.

Her girlfriends have been terrific in allowing Lisa to talk about her feelings as much as she's needed to. They have also consistently let her know that, when she is ready, they have a guy or two they'd like her to meet.

Last night one of her good friends called Lisa and asked her to a party she was giving Saturday night. Until now Lisa had been completely reluctant to take them up on any offers. And even now she's battling the temptation to tuck herself away in her room. But, thinking it over, Lisa has decided it's time to start joining the fun. She's tired of hiding and she feels she may be missing out on a lot. She agrees to go to the party, but as she hangs up the phone she's overwhelmed by anxiety. *I'm just not ready!* Lisa thinks desperately!

Any time you're hurt and retreat for a little while in order to recover, something other than a gentle mending takes place. A new pattern is formed. You become used to solitude, a lot of quiet thinking and the secure, safe (though sometimes sad) sensation of relying only on yourself.

But to give in to the security of not trusting or depending on anyone so as to avoid getting hurt is too easy to do, and terribly unfair to yourself. If you talk yourself out of it every time you're ready to open up, you could be setting yourself up for unnecessary, prolonged loneliness.

Of course it will be frightening! And there are no promises that you won't get hurt again. But new romance, light or serious, is too wonderful not to take a chance! If you don't, you'll be letting a past hurt run your life instead of being just a small part of it. When it's time to get out there, you'll know it. Don't let yourself think otherwise!

How Can I Get Myself to Go to a Party or Accept a Date When I'm So Afraid?

There are a few ways to put yourself in a better, or braver, state of mind.

Think about what you have to lose if you go out and have a bad time. Chances are you won't come up with much. A less than perfect evening may disappoint you, it may contribute to your fear that "there's no one out there," you may even feel a bit lonelier, but is any of this really *so* bad? Chalk it up to experience. After all, think of what you'd be facing if you stayed home: another evening of fear, another few hours to convince yourself you'll never get another boyfriend and another stretch of time in which those sensations of loneliness may take over. So don't stay home and let your fears get the best of you. Go out and take your chances—maybe you'll be pleasantly surprised!

Don't have expectations. Tell yourself that you are not going to the party or on the date to find "the one." You are going as a kind of experiment or exploration. It's time to leave your room and to start seeing the world again. What better way to do it than with a little companionship? This attitude will take the pressure off of you, and you won't feel the need to be accepted by your date as his future girlfriend.

You can start with a friendship and see where it goes from there. Besides, there's no reason to fall into a relationship so quickly. Give yourself some time to check out what's going on around you. After a good amount of time on your own, you'll know what the best choices for you are.

Concentrate on yourself. Carefully select your outfit, try a new makeup technique and perhaps wear your hair in a new, flattering way. There's nothing that can give you more confidence on a date or at a party than knowing you *look* terrific. Admiring glances and appreciative smiles will really help you feel more in control of your heart and far more confident in your ability to attract a new romantic partner.

Remember, most people experience fear when there is a risk. When you go out with your friends, you're never sure what's going to happen and how it will affect you. But think of it this way, the good things that could happen if you take a risk are *so* much more significant than the bad, that in a way, it's foolish to hesitate at all!

LOVE CYCLES

What if When I Emerge From Hiding, No One Is There?

Pamela's Story

I was so nervous! I hadn't joined my friends on a Friday or Saturday night for weeks. But suddenly there I was, itching to go out and terrified that no one would want to hear from me, I let an entire weekend go by, and finally it was Thursday night. I was practically shaking when I called my friend Bob. The last time I'd spoken to him we'd gotten into an argument because I didn't feel like playing our usual Saturday morning tennis game.

Well, I couldn't believe it! He was very surprised to hear from me and, though at first he was kind of quiet, when I told him I was feeling more like myself again he really perked up!

He's having a party Saturday night . . . and guess who's going?!

It's up to you! You are perfectly capable of expressing what you need. You just have to face it, and let others know:

- Try calling some friends and telling them that you think you're ready to start getting into the swing of things again. Let them know whether you're ready for a party, or perhaps even a date. See if they'd like to set you up with someone so that the four of you could go out together. Be open! If you've been a little to yourself lately, or unappreciative of people's efforts, admit it and apologize! Let your friends know what you need. They will come through!

- Explore a place or two on your own. Go to a local hangout or an intercollegiate sports competition and join in conversations with people you know. Act as open and as friendly as you possibly can. You could be quite surprised at how receptive people will be. In fact, sometimes walking into a place unaccompanied can be less threatening to those who notice than entering with a companion. They will probably assume that if you're on your own you may be more open to their introductions. And they will definitely be right!
- Join something! Try out for a team sport, become involved in a committee, volunteer for a fund raiser, or take an extra class in something you've always wanted to learn. A shared interest can be a wonderful springboard for friendship and romance.

- Give a party. Invite all of your friends and suggest that everyone bring someone new to the usual crowd. Parties which are filled with exciting strangers usually mean a good time for all. And throwing a party will speak for your re-entry into the social whirl!

The point is, if you come out of your cocoon and find the world is getting on quite well without you, *don't panic!* Just jump into the swing of things! With a little honesty, effort and courage you'll find yourself in step with everyone in no time.

I Feel Funny Letting Guys Know I'm Available Again, When I Know They Think I'm Either Still Involved or I Want to Be Alone. How Can I Tell Them Otherwise Without Being Too Obvious?

Naturally, it would feel very strange walking over to someone you're interested in and saying, "Hi there. I'm not involved anymore. Do you want to get to know me?" While frank remarks will always communicate the details of a situation or feeling very quickly, there are other ways to "signal" the same information.

Think in terms of "subtlety of expression." In other words, there's no need (unless of course you think it would be received well) to come right out and say exactly what you want. Too much forcefulness can put a person off. Just be yourself. People can sense from the way you look at them, stand near them and speak to them, whether or not you feel an attraction. And a few well chosen words will go a long way towards bringing you the desired results.

If you're talking to a cute guy at school who doesn't realize you've broken up with your ex:

- Mention it in passing. Work it into the conversation any way that seems most natural (even if it still does feel a little weird!). If he asks if you like to watch basketball games, say, "Oh, yes, Bill and I used to go all of the time before we broke up." If you're having trouble with some homework, try saying, "Bill used to help me with it, but now that we're not seeing each other anymore . . ." Don't be embarrassed! If he's interested, he'll be pleased to know you're available and your comments will seem like nothing more than fabulous news!

- If there's a casual event coming up, like a tennis match or a party, and you'd like this guy's company, try coming right out and saying, "You know, I'd love to watch the tennis game Saturday, but I'm not in the mood to go alone. Do you think you'd like to see it?" If he knows you were involved, he may ask you why you're not going to the game with your boyfriend. This will give you the perfect opportunity to explain that the two of you have broken up.
- Convince a friend to let him know! It's a bit cowardly, but you can only do what you feel comfortable doing! If you feel awkward, he may sense it, *and* misinterpret it. But if a friend delivers the message, he'll know for sure!

If you think the guy you're interested in doesn't know you're ready to start dating again, drop a few hints:

- Tell him about a movie you're dying to see but can't find anyone who is interested in going. If he doesn't pick up the hint, you can always casually add, "I don't suppose you'd like to see it?"
- If he's shown interest in you in the past but you've rebuffed his advances, remind him of an invitation he extended weeks

ago and say something like, "Can I take you up on that now?"
- Try coming right out and saying you're finally over Bill and are really looking forward to getting into the swing of things. (You needn't tell him how he fits into your new social picture. If he's interested, he'll find out!)

There are many ways to communicate availability. There's body language, facial expressions, warmth and words. You can be as direct or indirect as you feel comfortable and still make your point. Simply look for the opening, figure out what puts you at ease and decide what you think he'll feel comfortable hearing. Then say it and see what happens!

Your availability is good news for both of you, so make sure that *both* of you know about it!

I'm Afraid I Won't Give Anyone a Chance. Either He Won't Be Enough Like My Last Boyfriend, or He'll Be Too Much Like Him!

Every person you date will have their own unique personality. And while they may have some of the same qualities as your ex, good and

LOVE CYCLES

bad, this is no reason to fall for them instantly or to break up suddenly. Even though it's tempting, you can't isolate one or two characteristics of a person and rule out the rest of his personality. So be patient and get to know all there is about your partner. It might save you from a hasty decision you'll later regret!

There are a number of ways to help yourself get past the difficult expectations and fears with which you are now saddled. Here are a few tips to keep you from being your own worst enemy:

- Remember that your temptation to approach every guy in terms of how he compares to your ex is natural but unfair, so keep those expectations under control. Give him a chance. A *real* chance. Not just one disappointing date! It takes time to get to know somebody and for them to feel comfortable enough to show you their special sides.
- Don't expect too much emotional intimacy too fast. True, you've been used to a certain level of closeness in a relationship, but that level took months to create. It's unfair, even if your feelings of attraction are mutual, to expect the amount of intimacy to exist right away. Immediate intimacy can be very confusing and may even cause you to end a romance

that could have built into something even more significant than your last.

- Your date may do something that reminds you of a trait you didn't like in your ex. Don't look down on your date because of his actions. Your date and your ex are two different people who have their own set of reasons for doing what they do. Be cautious not to assign meaning to your date's actions until you get to know him better.

- If your date seems to possess all of the wonderful qualities you know you love, try to hold back from diving into the relationship head first. He *may* be "right" for you but, if you move too fast, your feelings will not have time to keep up the pace. You'll end up in an intense relationship that doesn't have enough emotional back-up, and the fear of too much sudden closeness could cause you to break up. And if he isn't right for you, by the time you figure it out you could be in so deep that you'll have to go through another breakup all over again. This is another example in which expecting too much too fast can leave you with a lot of hurt.

- Don't let yourself believe that great dates only exist in dreams. There will be times when there seems to be no one special

around to date, but let time run its course. When you least expect it, something wonderful will happen. You can't fall for everyone. If you did no one would be special and there would be very little excitement in your life.
- Let your more logical, less fearful side inspire you to give life a chance. Dating isn't always easy, but try to remind yourself that "You never know when something terrific will happen." Remember, things always look bad . . . until they begin looking good. Difficult times won't last forever, though it always seems as though they might. You *will* see the bad times fade away as new and positive things come into your life.
- And finally, aside from not expecting too much from the guys around you, *don't expect too much from yourself*. Breakups are difficult and take some serious getting over. Trusts can be broken, expectations ruined and dreams smashed. Allowing someone new into your life after getting over a major disappointment can be very difficult. Your emotions are not a revolving door in which people can come and go without your feeling their effect. So give yourself time to adjust and ready yourself for a new romance.

I'm Not Sure I Like the "Love Cycle." Moving Through a Wonderful Relationship Only to Have to Break Up and Start Again Is So Overwhelming!

It's true that the Love Cycle can feel overwhelming, but it's also true that there is nothing you can do about it. Unfortunately, like the old saying goes, "You have to take the good with the bad."

Anytime a meaningful romance ends, you're going to feel sad. But even in this sadness there lies a happy side. After all, you both know that what you had together was important, and that you really did and probably still do care.

Getting over the pain can be a slow and depressing process. But when it's all over, you'll be left feeling stronger, and surer of what you want and need.

Finally, finding a new romance after a breakup can be frightening because you don't want to get hurt again. But through experience you'll know a little more this time. Difficult times change people. They teach you coping strategies. Perhaps you will move through this new relationship more carefully, and if there is a breakup you will handle it more positively as well. And while, of course, there is no guarantee that you won't feel hurt again, it *will* be different. And from that difference, you will learn something new that will be helpful in the next romance . . . which there will surely be!

No, the Love Cycle isn't easy, but good things rarely are. If you want the best romance has to give, you have to be open to the problems that go with even the best of relationships!

There comes a time in the recovery from a breakup when you begin to give yourself signals—signals which indicate that it's time to let romance in once more. Suddenly, sitting home becomes more boring than secure; only seeing pals becomes less comforting and more confining. Movies, television and books no longer hold your attention as you begin eyeing the people around you.

Fear of more hurt may slow down the rate at which you get into the swing of things, and to a certain extent this serves as a useful shield. But don't let your fears get out of hand.

If you're tired of feeling rotten, then take charge! Go out and face the world. It has everything to offer. And when the road gets rocky, stay on it. Chances are it will still lead you to the wonderful excitement and pleasure you've been seeking!

Everything is a risk. But romance is usually worth it!

❤ CONCLUSION ❤

Love moves in cycles both within a single commitment and between relationships. Romance begins, grows and either ends—in which case a new romance begins—or it changes and grows in entirely new ways.

This constant movement is behind all successful romantic experiences. Every phase—the ups, the downs, the beginning, the middle *and the end*—represents a natural and healthy part of the love cycle.

Both blossoming romance and painful break-ups are positive signals. Their presence in your life mean you know how to care for someone and that you know how to be cared for. Even if someone changes in a way that seems to leave you behind, you will still know that you are capable of a lovely romance . . . and that another one is more than likely just around the bend!

Change, in general, can be hard to cope with. But change is what will keep your romance alive, or lead you to a new love that is even better than the last. So if you feel it taking over, grow with it. Don't hide. See where it takes you. And remember that love is a cycle. For every beginning there is an end. And for every end, a new beginning . . .

❤ NOTE FROM THE AUTHOR ❤

I have attempted in many different ways to show the simple, yet complicated; the painful, yet uplifting sides of breaking up. Much of how *you* experience a breakup will depend on you.

Your own needs and sensitivities can increase or alleviate the hurtful edge of a breakup. Your feelings are often what dictates whether your recovery will be quick or prolonged, and whether your subsequent relationships will be happy or not.

But despite the fact that breakups are experienced individually, there is one factor which remains constant for *everyone*: Breakups have the potential to become unbearable.

If for some reason a breakup seems too much to handle, it may be a signal that you need to talk to someone about it. Discussing your pain or confusion with an understanding counselor, either at school or at a clinic, can really help you climb out of what may feel like a *very* dark cloud. A broken heart is one of the most emotionally painful things anyone can experience. But it is an experience only. You shouldn't make it your whole life.

If you know you need help putting your breakup in its proper perspective, than do go out and ask for it. Along with all of love's ups and downs, *recovery* is another part of the Love Cycle that you really must allow yourself to experience.